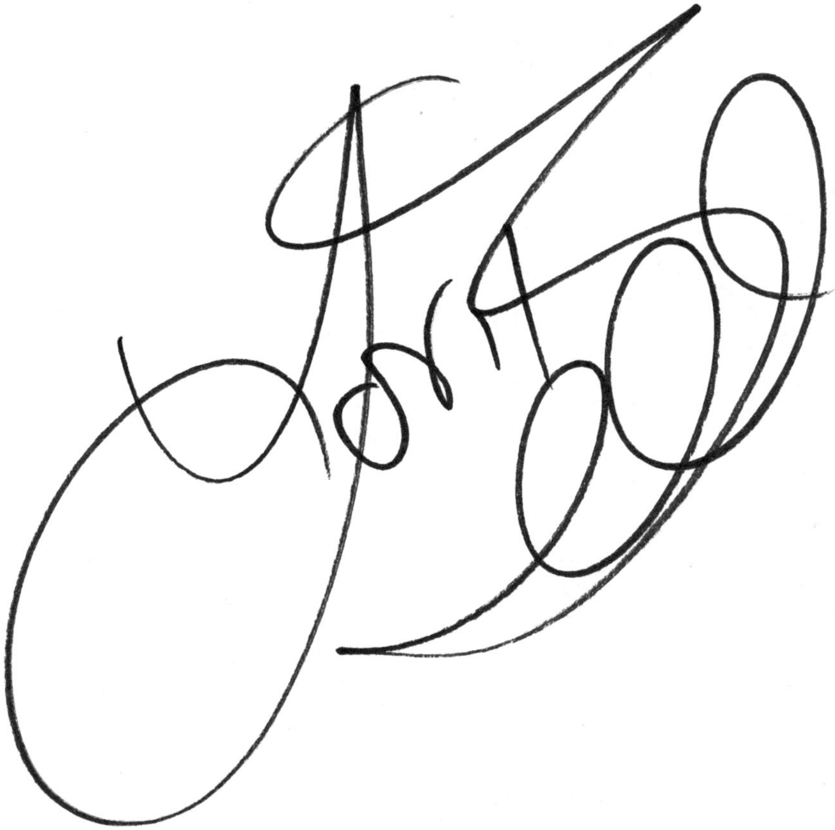

Trinity

Lori Bell

This book is a work of fiction. Names, characters, places and incidents are the product of the author's imagination or are used fictitiously. Any resemblance to actual events, locales, or persons, living or dead, is coincidental.

Copyright © 2017 by Lori Bell

All rights reserved. This book or any portion thereof may not be reproduced or used in any manner whatsoever without the express written permission of the publisher except for the use of brief quotations in a book review.

Cover photograph by CanStockPhoto

https://answers.yahoo.com/question/index;_ylt=AwrC2Q5Ss1pYuQYAglJPmolQ;_ylu=X3oDMTEzanFhbmlzBGNvbG8DYmYxBHBvcwMxMAR2dGlkA0IyNTU3XzEEc2VjA3Ny?qid=20081024042638AAIBVv8
https://en.wikipedia.org/wiki/Huntington%27s_disease
http://hddrugworks.org/dr-goodmans-blog/body-discomfort-and-pain-in-huntingtons

Printed by CreateSpace

ISBN 978 1542698375

DEDICATION

To everyone who wonders if I am writing about them. I am. I am inspired by people I know, and the stories I hear. Somewhere among the inspiration and the ideas, my creativity takes over. My belief is that I will never run out of stories about life. Because of all of you.

Chapter 1

In a kindergarten classroom in Lake Ozark, Missouri, there were two dozen children. Some were ready for the daily challenge of school. Smart. Outgoing. Social. Eager for knowledge. Others were still babies in countless ways. It depended upon their personalities, their genetics, and especially their environment at home. Precisely who those little people were at five and six years old already depicted so much of who they would become as adults.

Lizzy Thomas sat in the circle on the classroom floor. It was calendar time and she wished for it to be her turn to take the floor, stand up, and tell everyone it was Monday. Lizzy had brown eyes and long, thick dark brown hair with straight bangs. Her face was round and full, and her child-size body was as well. Chubby was adorable on her.

To Lizzy's right, seated in the circle on the blue and yellow swirl-patterned area rug, was Gianna Hunter, who preferred to be called Gi. Her auburn hair was cut into a sassy bob and her overgrown bangs often hung in her eyes. The headband she wore was useless. Gi never hesitated to express herself. Her likes *and* her dislikes. Her clothing style told so much about her already, when daily she donned bright colored tights –today's were orange– with a denim skirt, a matching denim jacket, and high-top tennis shoes with untied laces.

And to Lizzy's left was MacKenzie Wade, the blonde beauty with long hair perfectly twisted into a French braid. Her ruffled pink dress, white knee socks, and white patent shoes looked like she was well prepared for Easter Sunday.

Lizzy was proud to be sandwiched between those two girls. She thought of them as her friends, and often wrote their names along with hers on the backside of her homework papers. *Gi + Lizzy + Kenzie = Friends 4-Ever*. And sometimes, she added the word *Trinity*.

Since the beginning of the school year, just two months ago, the three of them regularly played together. Their preference was hopscotch outside on the playground during recess time. After weeks of doing this, a day came when Gi was distracted and wanted to leave them to play dodge ball with the boys. And then Kenzie was hesitant to scuff the bottoms of her new patent shoes – if she were to repeatedly jump on the rough concrete. Lizzy told them they were free to choose not to play with her. She promised them her feelings would not be hurt, because she knew they would always be there for each other. They were like a trinity. That was the first time Lizzy had told her friends what she believed was true.

"What's trinity?" Gi asked.

"Three close things, like family," Kenzie offered, because she had heard something about that once before on television.

"Yes," Lizzy agreed with Kenzie's explanation, and smiled because she was proud of her analogy of them. *The three of them. And their closeness.* "It also means God, his son – Jesus, and the Holy Spirit in my church." Lizzy was exceptionally wise beyond her years. A prodigy. And she already knew the value of having true friends.

"I am not churchie, so I'm not a part of a trinity," Gi stated, in a matter-of-fact tone.

"Remember, it's also three close things. Nothing to do with church." Lizzy smiled wide, showing her missing two front teeth on the top row. Lizzy wholeheartedly believed she and her friends exemplified trinity.

✱

Lizzy sat at the kitchen table in the lakefront house she shared with her parents and two-year-old brother. She had homework to complete tonight, and she was excited about it. They were finally working on writing and were now printing the upper and lowercase letter L in her kindergarten class. L was for Lizzy, and Lizzy of course had already mastered writing her entire name –first, middle, and last– not long after she turned four years old.

Her father, John Thomas, was sitting at the table beside her, watching her skillfully move her number two pencil. "Perfect. Just perfect," he told her twice, beaming with pride. Her mother, Kara Thomas was upstairs. She had gone to sleep right after she tucked Lizzy's little brother, Lance into bed. It was a way of life for all of them. Lizzy, especially, was accustomed to her mother always being tired.

✱

MacKenzie Wade pushed her dinner plate forward. Grilled filet mignon, baked potato, and French-style green beans. She had barely touched any of it. She would have rather had spaghetti or pizza, like her friends were allowed to eat. Her parents were too excessively wrapped up in each other to ever notice her disappointment in anything. And, right now, they were too engulfed in their conversation to see MacKenzie had left the room. They were talking about a larger and fancier home they wanted to buy. MacKenzie didn't want to move again. She and her parents had only lived in their house in Lake Ozark for two years. MacKenzie liked it there. She hoped, if they did move again, it would be just to a new house, not a new city. She couldn't bear the thought of leaving her friends. Lizzie and Gi were very special to her.

*

Gi Hunter sat on the floor in front of the TV with a half-eaten peanut butter and jelly sandwich in her hand. Her mother was working late again, waitressing. She didn't have a father. She had never even met the man who was absent from her life before she was even born – as her mother, Dixie Hunter would say. Gi lived with her mother and her seventeen-year-old brother. He was in the back bedroom of their doublewide trailer right now with his girlfriend, doing God knows what to make his bed squeak like that again. Gi turned up the volume on the television set and took another bite of the sandwich she had fixed herself for dinner, for the third consecutive evening.

✱

At school the next day, Lizzy, Gi, and Kenzie were in the classroom, seated at their desks, pushed together into a quad. There was one seat empty among theirs. That classmate had contracted the chicken pox.

"So do you think we will get those pox, too, since we sit by Sally every day?" Kenzie asked her friends, already scratching her arm because the mere thought of it made her itch.

"I've already had 'em," Lizzy stated, "and once you have 'em you can't get 'em back."

"Not true," Gi interjected. "My brother had chicken pox twice, but I'm immune to them. That means the virus does not affect my body."

Both Lizzy and Kenzie nodded their heads, having learned something new already, and the bell had not even rung yet for the school day to begin in Mrs. Diercks' classroom.

"We might be moving," Kenzie stated outright.

"Where? Like somewhere far?" Lizzy asked, instantly worried about this.

"I think it's just to a bigger house in our same town," Kenzie said. "I couldn't understand much of what my parents were talking about last night, and I didn't ask questions because they hardly knew I was there again."

"I know the feeling," Gi chimed in. "Being at my house with my brother and his girlfriend is just like being alone. They lock his bedroom door a lot."

"That's probably because they are kissing, you know, like in the movies when they never stop. And they use tongues," Lizzy stated all knowingly, and the girls giggled in unison.

"My parent kiss like that," Kenzie added.

"Mine don't. Probably because mom is always sleeping," Lizzy said, almost nonchalantly. It didn't make her feel as sad anymore. She was just used to it. Her father took care of her, and she tried very hard to help him take care of her little brother. They all did what they had to do. *For mommy.*

"Will your mom ever start feeling better? I mean, what does the doctor say?" Kenzie asked, and she and Gi both stared at Lizzy. Waiting for her to answer.

"She's just going to get sicker." Lizzy looked down when she spoke those words, and both Gi and Kenzie moved closer to her. Gi placed her hand, palm down, on the middle of the joined desktops between them. Kenzie placed her hand on top of Gi's. And last, Lizzy did the same on the very top. That one simple gesture was an indescribable comfort. It was the closeness between them that always made everything feel all right.

✱

The three of them rode their bicycles from Kenzie's golf course home. It had been five years since Kenzie's family moved into an even more spacious, fancier home in a gated subdivision overlooking a golf course that meandered through two hundred and fifty acres of Ozark forest, meadows and scenic valleys along Little Bear Creek. The girls, now all ten years old, followed Lizzy's lead as they pedaled into the city cemetery. They ended up there often. It's just what Lizzy needed to do. And she always wanted both Gi and Kenzie to accompany her.

They slowed their bicycles, got off, and tipped them on their sides in the grass on the ground close to Kara Thomas' gravestone. As she always did, Lizzy walked up there first. She had doubled her height in the past five years, and she continued to tip the scale on the higher end.

"Did I ever tell you two that it helps for me to look at her picture on there?" Lizzy asked, pointing to the photograph sealed behind an oval shape of thick glass. It was Lizzy's mother's graduate of nursing school photograph. She was young, vibrant, and beautiful then. And a picture of health at that time. Neither Gi nor Kenzie had ever seen her look that way.

"Don't you have any pictures of her at home?" Kenzie asked, running her fingers through her long, blonde, wind-blown hair. She wished she had brought a hair tie with her around her wrist, in case she would have needed one on the bike ride, or now standing in the blustery open air. She didn't like feeling disheveled.

"Some, on my dresser in my room, but my dad put all of the others away. It's painful for him. That's also why he doesn't bring me and my brother here. Lance doesn't even remember her. I really can't talk about my mom at home. That's why I come here with you both."

"Anytime you need to," Gi began, looking down at the grassy ground and then back up at Lizzy, "I will do this with you." Gi's bangs were in her eyes again. Her thick auburn tresses were long on top, but closely shaved up the base of her neck. She was only ten years old, but already had a bold haircut –and mindset– like a teenager.

"Me too," Kenzie agreed, wishing she was more like Gi and could speak her mind and express herself so openly.

"I know," Lizzy sighed as she knelt down on the ground and ran her fingers overtop of the black-marbled headstone.

✤

Lizzy, Gi, and Kenzie all turned sixteen consecutively in June, July, and August. They were inseparable now, more than ever, given that their independence was amplified with driver's licenses.

It was the last Saturday night in August before their junior year of high school would begin. Lizzy was behind the wheel of her father's full-size SUV. Of the threesome, she was already the most responsible driver. And because they all had just come from a teen party at the home of one of their classmates whose parents were out of town for the weekend, it was best that Lizzy was driving. Considering she was the only one of the three of them who did not drink alcohol tonight.

Kenzie was sitting in the passenger seat beside Lizzy. She sat very still with her head back and her eyes closed. The concoction in her stomach of vodka, wine, and beer was not settling well. And the movement of the vehicle made her feel more nauseated by the second. She took a few deep breaths. And when Gi started talking in the backseat, Kenzie was able to keep her mind off of feeling sick.

"You know what, girls?" Gi's voice was louder and considerably more boisterous than usual. "A person hasn't lived until they've sipped enough alcohol to feel tipsy!"

"So, of the three of us, I have yet to *live*?" Lizzy asked Gi, in a snarky tone, as she glanced into her rearview mirror in the dark vehicle but could not see Gi behind her. Gi giggled and Kenzie snickered under her breath, still with her eyes closed and head back. But Lizzy ignored them both when she briefly turned around to find Gi lying down on the backseat. "What are you doing?"

"Resting. This vehicle is like a house on wheels – it's roomier than my trashy trailer anyway. I'm enjoying the ride, Liz." Gi was past the point of tipsy. She was drunk. And this wasn't the first time.

"I will give you three seconds to sit up and buckle your seatbelt or I'm pulling over and not moving until you do!" Lizzy was adamant and she immediately slowed her speed.

"Yeah, yeah," Gi said, obeying Lizzy's request, but not without complaint. "What is with you anyway? When will the day come for you to break a few rules?" Kenzie opened her eyes and looked to her left at Lizzy. This was always an issue among them. Gi broke rules. Kenzie had a good girl image, but she teetered on the line and often made risky choices, but always covered her tracks well. Lizzy was the responsible, straight arrow of the three of them. Until tonight.

While the party was going on, both Gi and Kenzie noticed Lizzie having a casual conversation with Trey Toennies, the star basketball player at Osage High School. He was about to be a senior. He looked like a man, not a boy of eighteen. Broad shoulders, thick chest, dark hair, blue eyes. Neither Gi nor Kenzie were aware that Lizzie had gone upstairs with him.

Lizzy and Trey were talking about the pressure to drink. Trey's father died of acute alcohol poisoning at just thirty-three years old. Trey, as a result, was afraid to touch a drop of it. Lizzy told him she understood. Not so much did she have apprehension about alcohol, but she did know all too well what it was like to lose a parent. Her mother had been gone for ten years of her life already. Lizzy and Trey found an easy connection. And when he kissed her in the far corner of the basement, her world changed. She had never been kissed by a boy before. She often felt too self conscious not being a size two or four like Gi and Kenzie. She rarely found the confidence to flirt. But, with Trey, it was different. She had not thought once about how she looked or what she was saying. Everything just felt effortless with him. Especially kissing him. He led her upstairs to one of the empty bedrooms and on a stranger's bed, Lizzy had lost her virginity at sixteen.

She was still reeling with the wonder and awe of what had happened as she drove Gi and Kenzie home. They were her two closest friends in the world. They all were more like sisters. Lizzy should have blurted out by now what she had experienced. There was just one problem. One very important thing standing in the way and keeping her from sharing her secret. Trey was Kenzie's boyfriend.

*

With this ring I thee wed. "Who says *thee* anyway?" Gi leaned into Lizzy and whispered as they both suppressed a giggle. Side by side, with their elbows touching at times, they stood on a wide dock overlooking the Lake of the Ozarks. Their lilac matching matron of honor gowns were strapless and reached their ankles, just above their white strappy stilettos. They were grown women now. Twelve years had passed, and at twenty-eight years old, Gi, Lizzy, and Kenzie remained locked in lasting friendship.

Gi brushed the hair out of her eyes with her fingers, as the warm spring wind picked up near the water. She still kept her auburn hair short, a few generous inches above the back of her neckline. She wore it longer and full on top, where it was parted wildly and unevenly chic on one side, leaving her long bangs to often cover one of her eyes, depending on the part. She still teetered between a size two and four with very little effort. She consumed any food she desired and exercise was foreign to her. She had good genes, Gi liked to say, and would credit her mother for those. But, that was all she ever gave her mother any recognition for. Throughout most of her adult life, Gi had preferred to remain a little estranged from Dixie Hunter. Their conversations, infrequent and far from warm and heartfelt, were now just civil at most.

Gi looked out into the flock of people, seated on white chairs, aligned row after row on the dock. She saw a man slouching a bit in his chair. He maintained short ash brown hair with a neatly trimmed goatee on his boyish face. He wore a khaki suit, a white shirt open wide at the collar, sans the tie. And brown leather flip flops were on his feet just because. Ric Sutter didn't follow a dress code or rules of any type. He was his own man, and he was also Gi's man. And how ironic it was as Gi witnessed one of her best friends gaining a husband today, she wished she could lose hers.

Gi and her husband appeared to be a well-matched couple. A wild girl and a bad boy. But, as it turned out, their union had created too much fire and too much friction. It also had produced the little girl seated next to her daddy right now with untamed auburn hair, a short ruffled white dress and pink high-top tennis shoes. Suzie was five years old, and was the light of Gi's life. She would have done absolutely anything for her. And right now she was keeping their family together. Gi knew all too well what it was like to grow up without a father. In her eyes, Dixie Hunter had done nothing to keep her father in her life. Gi believed that, and she realized her resentment toward her mother stemmed from it. The one thing she could never handle would be causing her little girl that same kind of pain. So, Gi felt fiercely constrained to call herself Mrs. Ric Sutter.

Lizzy glanced down at her cleavage spilling out of the top of her strapless dress. She battled with her weight all of her life, but despite her full figure, she was stunningly gorgeous. Her long, dark hair was in an updo today and her dark eyes, full lashes, perfect cheekbones, and pouty lips could have easily passed her off as the baby sister of Angelina Jolie.

A burly man, twenty years her senior, was smiling at Lizzy from a spot among the sea of white chairs. Max Zurliene was a broad-chested, big round bellied man with thinning, moderately graying hair that was once jet black. He had been nothing but good, honest and loving to Lizzy since the day she met him. That was ten years ago when she was a single mother and scared. The high school jock, Trey Toennies had wanted no part of taking responsibility for the baby he fathered the night Lizzy had lost her virginity to him. He was going to college on a basketball scholarship. He didn't have any room in his life for a baby. Lizzy's father helped her raise her baby for two years. And when Lizzy was eighteen, she married Max. She married him for the security he had promised her. *Did she love him?* No. But he adored her. And her baby boy, who was now *their* preteen son. If Lizzy had learned anything about life –and marriage– it was when you act as if you love someone day after day, year after year, you see all of their faults, shortcomings, and quirks, and you learn to accept them as they are. Max Zurliene was Lizzy's husband and she cared deeply about him without judgment.

Kenzie wore the same strappy white stilettos as her matrons of honor. Her dress was cap-sleeved and pure lace. It hugged tightly around her curvy figure, and the generous slit almost entirely up the one side of the dress, accented her long legs. Her blonde hair was down, flowing in bouncy, loose curls.

Kenzie was picture perfect on any day, but especially on her wedding day. Of she, Gi, and Lizzy, Kenzie was the one determined to marry for love. And today she had.

First, Kenzie watched Lizzy marry too young and honor her vows to a man she didn't love – for the sake of giving her baby a loving father and a financially secure life. Then, Kenzie witnessed Gi fall hard for a man she shared an intense passion with, but once the novelty of their physical attraction subsided, the fighting completely took over their relationship and suffocated their love. It was going to be different for Kenzie. Marriage would be about spending her days and nights beside the one person she could not imagine her life without. For Kenzie, that person was Peter Sterling. He was a successful business man with fortune and prestige. And physically, he was built like a stone statue model in a museum full of faultless bodies. The only thing wrong and unbearably sad was Peter had just six months to live. And only he and Kenzie knew.

Chapter 2

"So, you think six months is long enough?" Gi asked Kenzie as the two of them stood close along with Lizzy in their usual half circle stance – still dressed elegantly with champagne glasses in hand. The wedding reception was in full celebratory mode under a large white tent in the grass just a short distance away from the dock overlooking the water.

"Excuse me?" Kenzie asked, feeling her own eyes widen as she glanced past Gi and over at her husband, mingling with their guests not too far from them. She suddenly wanted to be by his side, making sure he was feeling strong enough to tackle this long day. Their special day.

"You know, to date, get engaged, and tie the knot," Gi stated, and then she broke into a grin. "I'm kidding, Kenz! It's obvious how much you two adore the hell out of each other and I think the three of us know your marriage will outlast all of ours in the happiness department when it's all said and done." Lizzy rolled her eyes, and Kenzie inhaled a deep breath and tried to smile. *If only her husband would be given the chance.*

"Stop looking so serious," Lizzy chimed in and took a hold of Kenzie's arm. "Gi is just being Gi. She can't help it she's an asshole." They giggled, and in turn, Gi took a sip of her champagne and then spit it into Lizzy's glass.

"As I said, asshole!" Lizzy poured out her drink in the grass behind them. No matter their age or where they were present together, they were trinity. As close as three people could possibly be.

✱

Gi tucked her little girl into bed well after midnight. She had danced the night away on the makeshift dance floor under the large white tent at the wedding reception, only getting sleepy on their less than ten-minute ride home. Gi helped her out of her pink high-top tennis shoes and then the white ruffled dress. She slipped an oversized florescent pink t-shirt overtop her head, and when Suzie sleepily inserted her arms into it, the size of the shirt swallowed her up. Gi smiled. Her daughter was hardly a girlie-girl. It had been a fight earlier today just to get her to wear a dress, especially one with ruffles, which was exactly why Gi never objected to the pink high-tops. That little girl was no doubt just like her mama. Not at all frilly. Gi kissed her small forehead, told her she loved her more than anything, and Suzie already had her eyes closed when she sunk her head into her pillow and mumbled, "I love you too, mommy."

Gi closed the door to her daughter's bedroom and walked barefoot down the hallway on the dark hardwood flooring. Wearing her strapless bridesmaid's dress, she smiled to herself at the thought of Kenzie being married. She was the last of the three of them to get hitched, and while Gi didn't think too much of marriage –based on her own– she knew Kenzie was happy. And Gi was happy for her and Peter.

When she reached the end of the hallway, she turned into the open doorway of her bedroom. Ric was already lying on their bed, shirtless and barefoot, but still wearing his khaki suit pants. Gi had driven them home tonight, because Ric had been intoxicated. It wasn't blatantly obvious to anyone else at the wedding reception, at least Gi didn't think so, as Ric was not boisterous or obnoxious when he drank too much. But Gi could always tell. Ironically, he was nicer to her when he consumed alcohol.

"Hey baby," Rick spoke to her with a wide smile, and drunk, wanting eyes. "Come lay by me."

"No thanks, I'm going to take a shower," Gi replied, walking over to her dresser to retrieve a pair of panties and a t-shirt from the top drawer.

"What the hell?" he stated, jumping off the bed, planting his feet on the floor, and making his way quickly over to her before she could turn around and take a few steps toward their master bathroom. His face was close to hers. So close she could smell the vodka on his breath. "We should be celebrating…your soul sister got married today." Ric often mocked Gi's bond with Kenzie and Lizzy. "Come on, come to bed." Ric cupped her breast peeking from her strapless dress and forcefully planted his lips on his wife's. Gi felt her body tense. She immediately pushed off of his bare chest with the palms of her hands. "Don't be a dick, Ric," was all she said to her husband as she brushed past him and closed and locked the bathroom door behind her.

*

Lizzy passed by the open doorway of her son's room. He was sitting on the foot end of his bed, with his cell phone in hand. He had gone to the wedding ceremony today, but did not stay for the reception after dinner. At twelve years old, he was bored unless he was with his friends – or on his phone.

"Good night, Grif," Lizzy said, leaning in the doorway, now wearing her worn out white terrycloth robe because she could not wait to get out of her dress. She didn't remember the last time she pranced around with her boobs half hanging out. Gi had teased her about it, too, because Lizzy was definitely the most conservative of the three of them. "Thank you for coming with us today. I know Kenzie appreciated having you there. She loves you, honey." When Griffin was born, the girls were all almost seventeen years old. Lizzy having a baby that young had affected each of them. Baby Grif had become so special. He bonded with the girls, and without a doubt he always knew he was loved. Kenzie and Gi, however, learned firsthand and very quickly the importance of using birth control. They knew for certain they did not want the responsibility of a baby too soon.

"I know," Griffin replied, somewhat embarrassed, but touched. Like his mother, Griffin had dark hair, striking facial features, and a thick body.

Lizzy left Griffin's room on the second floor and then headed up another flight of stairs to the master suite she shared with her husband. Their house was immense, their cars were always new, and their life was better than comfortable. They had never had any children together. Only Griffin, whom they raised when Max adopted him and gave him his name and so much more. He provided well for Lizzy and her son. There was no spark between Lizzy and her husband, but their love was genuine. And, for Lizzy, that was enough. Or at least it had been for the past twelve years.

Max's successful career as an attorney allowed Lizzy to never work a day in her life. She finished high school and didn't attend college. She got married when all of her friends went off to college. With a toddler, there wasn't time for Lizzy to go to college. Or, at least that was the notion Max had put into her head. Lizzy's father, however, tried to no avail to get her to change her mind. *You'll regret it one day*, he had told her. And that day had come.

At twenty-eight years old, Lizzy had accomplished nothing for herself. Her son was growing up and needing her less and less. He was now at the awkward preteen age where being with his mother was embarrassing, especially when his friends were present. Lizzy knew when to back off and how to give her son his space. She had more alone time on her hands already at this stage in her life, and it had gotten her thinking. Especially after she met Hank Stewart.

Lizzy greatly enjoyed gardening, planting flowers, and landscaping. Just two months ago when the weather broke, she had gone to Plant Land in Lake Ozark. The store specialized in landscape design, but Lizzy just enjoyed browsing in the garden center and choosing her own plants, flowers, and landscape accessories. She had an eye for it. And that was precisely what the new owner, Hank Stewart had told her when she met him in the store for the first time just seven weeks ago.

He was about her age, Lizzy knew, because she remembered him from high school. She also knew he was divorced. Most people's personal lives were an open book in Lake Ozark. His hair was so blond it almost appeared white and his skin always looked just the right amount of sunkissed. Not too overbaked and hardly fair. Lizzy had shaken off how much he had affected her the first time she met him. But, each meeting with him thereafter had added fuel to a foreign fire.

The last time they were together, Lizzy had gotten so caught up in the connection she found with this man over landscape design that she hired him to redo her entire yard. Hank wasn't the type of businessman to be kind in order to sell his product. He was genuine and knowing the home and yard that was Lizzy's, he was excited to take on the creative opportunity to enhance the beauty of an already breathtaking home.

Lizzy laid in bed right now, next to her snoring husband, and she could hardly wait another day until Monday morning when Hank would arrive. It was completely innocent, Hank had become her friend, she reminded herself again as she rolled her back to her husband's and closed her eyes.

✱

Kenzie's knees were bent and her palms were open, both sinking into the king-size mattress of the bed she was sharing tonight with the man she could now call her husband. Peter was behind her, hard and thrusting inside of her. "Oh God, oh God, oh God!" he cried out with his release, and Kenzie fell forward onto her pillow. Peter followed her, and spooned her body with his.

There were tears streaming down Kenzie's face that she didn't want him to see. But, he knew her well. "Hey, babe, we agreed no sadness. We have a lot of memories to pack into a little time."

"I know," Kenzie agreed, as she choked on a cry. But she cursed how unfair this was.

"Today was wonderful, and I know this sounds cheesy, but it really was the happiest day of my life," Peter told his wife, as she rolled onto her back and then turned her body into his. Their faces were only inches apart.

"Mine, too," she spoke clearly, despite how she was still fighting back tears. For him. For them. For the future they would never have. "I didn't expect us to be able to do this tonight," she giggled a little. "I thought you would be too tired."

"Too tired to make love to the sexiest, most beautiful woman I'm able to call my wife? I think not," Peter said, moving in to kiss her tenderly on the lips, and she combed her fingers through his wavy brown hair.

"Are you in any pain?" Kenzie asked, when their lips parted.

"Nothing the pain meds can't take care of," Peter stated, but Kenzie knew he had not taken anything, because when he did, he had no appetite and he quickly became fatigued. She watched him both eat and drink today during their wedding celebration, so she knew he was tolerating, not appeasing, any pain. She had prayed for God to give him this day – pain free. It was their wedding day, and if this God had planned to take her husband away from her in just a few short months, that was the least he could do. Kenzie felt cynical and it was destroying her not to be able to talk to Lizzie and Gi about this. Lizzie had gone through losing her mother and she had faced the merciless pain of grief. And Lizzie had come out stronger and more faithful than ever. Gi was altogether different. Her humor and cynicism, combined with incredible strength, had powered her through the tough times in her life. Kenzie needed both of her girlfriends for those reasons and more, but she had promised Peter to keep his illness –and its devastating prognosis – between them.

Chapter 3

When the white landscaping truck with green *Plant Land* lettering pulled up and parked along the curb in front of her house, Lizzy was peering out of her front window with her first cup of morning coffee in hand. She had changed clothes twice, and finally told herself while looking in the mirror that she was being *ridiculous*.

Should I let him ring the doorbell and come inside? Or should I nonchalantly go out there? She was a married woman acting like an anxious, giddy teenager. And while she recognized how wrong it was on many accounts, this feeling intrigued her. So much so, she opened her front door and walked down the sidewalk to greet him.

Hank had just gotten out of his truck and was making his way around the full length of the trailer behind it. He glanced at the house, and on the sidewalk he saw her. "Good morning, Elizabeth," he smiled. He liked calling her Elizabeth and he had started to just weeks after they had met. Lizzy was touched when he said his late grandmother's name was the same.

"Good morning to you," she said, reaching the end of the sidewalk where he met her. He was wearing denim, brown work boots, and a white t-shirt that hugged his torso and biceps. Lizzy wore a full-length lime green sundress with a three-quarter-length crocheted white sweater over top, with white flip flops on her feet. She had just gotten a pedicure and her nails, fingers and toes, were painted pale pink. She sometimes dwelled on how she was chunky, but today she felt pretty. Hank had something to do with that. She tried not to stare at his thick, muscular frame.

"I didn't know if you would be home or not, but I'm happy you are," he spoke honestly, and her insides fluttered something fierce. "I'll be trimming and extracting a few things in the front yard before I bring in what you and I chose for the new look." All Lizzy heard from that statement was *you and I*. She listened to him finish speaking, solely about the landscape, and she tried harder to pay attention this time. When he started walking up toward the house, Lizzy was in step with him. But, she stopped when another car pulled up to her house, this one on the driveway. It was Gi. Lizzy cursed her timing, as she met her on the driveway where Gi stepped out of her burnt orange colored jeep. She was wearing skinny khaki pants, dark brown wedges, and her cap-sleeved top was the same burnt orange color as the jeep.

"Do you always match your clothes with your vehicle?" Lizzy teased her. It wasn't unusual for Gi to stop by unannounced. This time, she was on her way to work. Gi owned a gift shop downtown Lake Ozark. It was a store with everything from fine jewelry to t-shirts and souvenirs. Vacationers to the lake absolutely loved it, which allowed Gi to make a decent living. She had earned a bachelor's degree in business management with an emphasis in ownership and had put her college education to perfect use.

"Do you always flirt with the hired help?" Gi had purposely kept her voice low, and she giggled when she saw Lizzy's reaction. Her eyes widened and her face flushed before she shushed Gi with a scowl on her face.

"Do not call someone hired help. It's demeaning and rude. He owns Plant Land and he's redoing our landscaping," Lizzy sounded annoyed as she explained.

"Oh yes, it's high time. What an eye sore your weeds in front of this mansion have been." Gi teased, and remembered Lizzy had spoken of their landscape redo, but was certain she had not mentioned *Hank*.

Lizzy cut her off. "Did you stop by for something specific because I'm really not in the mood for your sarcasm?"

"Well I just could not help it. Here I was driving by and I saw you dolled up in a dress and your body language screamed something along the lines of flirting…I had to stop to see what's up with you." Gi's curiosity had peaked. She could never remember seeing Lizzy like this. *Smitten*. And that's because she hadn't been. The first boy she kissed, she slept with and became pregnant. The next man who paid attention to her, she married.

It was no secret between the three friends that Lizzy, at eighteen years old, made a rash commitment to Max Zurliene because she was scared, immature, and mostly because his offer was too good –and too safe– to refuse.

"I'm not talking to you about this now." This time Lizzy purposely kept her voice low.

"So there *is* something going on?" Gi's eyes widened. Lizzy shrugged her shoulders. "Your silence is a dead giveaway. And, you know, if Kenz wasn't on her honeymoon I would drag her over here for an intervention."

"What are you trying to save me from?" Lizzy asked.

"Making a mistake, maybe?" Gi offered.

"Can we talk later?" Lizzy asked, glancing up at the house where Hank was already on his hands and knees in the landscape rocks. Maybe she did need to confess this.

"You know where to find me," Gi spoke, as she turned to get back inside of the jeep. "And, Lizzy?" Lizzy walked closer to the open jeep door. "I've never seen you like this before. This clearly isn't you. Be careful…and I'm not just saying that because I love you. I'm warning you that sometimes our feelings can get us into some serious trouble."

"You're scaring me a little," Lizzy admitted.

"Not as much as you're scaring me," Gi replied, and she turned over the engine and backed out of the driveway.

Kenzie sat across the table from her husband at the Kihei Café in Maui. It was the third day of their Hawaiian honeymoon. Aside from Peter having slept the entire eight-hour flight there, Kenzie hardly noticed if he was struggling to keep up with her on the vacation they had both dreamed of experiencing.

The involuntary movement of his eyelid caught Kenzie's attention as she took a bite of her vegetable and cheese omelet and watched Peter cut into the steak on his plate, moving the medium-well cooked meat against a heaping pile of scrambled eggs. He was focused on the back and forth sawing of his knife, while talking and purposely ignoring the twitching going on above his eye. *What was Kenzie to do? Ignore it, too?* She knew from having done her own extensive research on Huntington's Disease that there would be slight, uncontrollable muscular movements. Among other signs. Most were things all people did occasionally. Like, stumbling and clumsiness. Lack of concentration. Short-term memory lapses. Depression or changes of mood. Kenzie did know what Peter fretted and obsessed about the most. He feared exhibiting aggressive behavior. He witnessed both his grandfather and later his father become bad-tempered too many times from the effects of the disorder that was indeed inherited.

From the time he was a young boy, Peter knew of HD as the death of brain cells. He was aware of how losing those brain cells affected mood, coordination, and even speaking. His grandfather was only in his early fifties when the disease robbed him of his ability to talk. And, after that, he had given up on his life and only lived a couple more years. Peter's father, on the other hand, never stopped talking. Or yelling. And Peter's mother had not been able to live her life like that after years of being on the receiving end of the abuse. She divorced him, and Peter never saw his father again. Peter was ten years old when his parents separated, and fifteen when his father died. His father was one of the seven percent of those affected with HD who had taken his own life.

There was no cure for the disease that can plague both men and women, with its onset usually between the ages of thirty and fifty. Peter was thirty-two, just six months ago, when he was officially diagnosed. He had been obsessively watching for the signs throughout most of his adult life. His early and immediate diagnosis unfortunately changed nothing. In fact, doctors had found a faster progression of the symptoms in Peter. His life expectancy could be as long as fifteen years or as short as one year. Peter was already halfway through the one year that the doctors were certain he only had left.

"Are you even listening to me?" Peter asked, interrupting Kenzie's devastating thoughts. She was moving her fork around on her plate, gradually tearing apart the omelet but not making any effort to eat it.

"What? Yes. I'm sorry." It sickened her, knowing this was their first and last beautiful trip they would ever take together.

"We are hiking the side of Black Rock cliff today. It's three miles up to the top. You need to eat for energy." Peter was excited about their plan, but Kenzie was worried about him. *Physically, could he really endure that?* He didn't have to prove anything to her. She already believed him to be super human.

"What about you?" Kenzie asked him. "What about your energy level? Let's not get crazy, Peter."

"Crazy?" he asked her, feeling like it was time for him to pump her up. To prepare her for how tough she needed to be. Especially after he was gone. "Crazy is sitting around dwelling and crying over something we cannot change. I have one life. You have one life. We got married to join our lives and no matter how much time anyone has left, it should be about soaking up every moment. Humor me, please. If I stumble today, I'm a klutz anyway, everyone knows that. If I need to stop halfway up to catch my breath, rest my body, or close my eyes, let me do that with you by my side. Because… today we have all the time in the world."

Kenzie reached across the table for his hand and held it. "Give me five minutes to clean my plate so I can climb that cliff with my husband."

Below the cliff hikers were a few swimmers snorkeling the big wall dubbed Black Rock. While Kenzie and Peter made their way up the trail with some steep turns, and large rocks, she reached for his hand more than a few times when he would stumble or slow his pace. The sun was warm and they talked about witnessing others along their hike who were there for cliff jumping. Some of the locations were off limits for jumping or diving. There were red flags and temporary railings to alert people of the dangerous conditions.

"Why are some of these spots off limits?" Kenzie asked as she watched Peter lean his back up against one of the railings and reach into his backpack to retrieve bottles of water for them.

"Large underwater rocks or inadequate water depth," Peter answered her. He had done his research before taking his wife up there.

"Are we going to look for a safe area with lower height and deeper water and just do it?" Kenzie asked him, and he smiled wide at her. One of the many things he loved about her was her sense for adventure.

"Seriously? It would be nice to cool off…" Peter stated, not having thought they would cliff jump today. What he really wanted to do was find an area along their hike where no one else was around, so he could talk to her. It was time for him to tell her how scared he was to fight this disease and to lose his life. A life he was unfairly just beginning with her. She needed to know how much he didn't want to leave her.

"We can see if you feel up to it once we're on our way down," Kenzie suggested, as she watched him place his backpack on the ground before he sat down and leaned up against the railing. His khaki cargo shorts hugged his muscular quads, his red t-shirt was damp from perspiration. He stretched his legs out in front of him and Kenzie noticed one of them repeatedly shaking from below his hip socket all the way down to the hiking boot on his foot.

"You okay?" she asked him, wasting no time to sit down beside him. She reached out to gently rub his leg, in an attempt to calm the shaking.

"No, we both know I'm not okay." Peter looked forlorn as Kenzie studied his face. For the first time since he told her of his diagnosis and its awful prognosis, she saw real sadness –and possibly even a loss of hope– in his eyes.

"I told you we shouldn't have done this hike," Kenzie began, but Peter interrupted.

"That's not what I mean. I want to do this with you. I brought you up here for a reason. Just hear me," he asked of her. Kenzie's blonde hair was pulled high on top of her head in a long, thick ponytail. Both the color and the fitted style of her yellow tank top accented her tan skin, and full chest. She wore frayed denim cut offs and tan hiking boots. She was the type of woman who could slip into a paper sack and make it look sexy. Looking at her made Peter's heart swell. She was his. But it pained him knowing not for long.

"I grew up watching this disease destroy the only two males in my life. When it was all said and done and it had ravaged their bodies, their souls were gone too. They were no longer men to be proud of. I don't want to be them." Peter took a moment to catch his breath, and Kenzie never spoke a word, nor took her focus off of him. "I will do anything for you not to have to feed me, or try to read my mind because I can no longer speak and my hands are shaking too badly to write. And I swear to you, I will not lash out in anger because I've turned into some kind of angry psychotic fucker. That's not me, and it will not be me."

"Peter, stop," Kenzie tried to interject.

"No, you need to hear this. And I need to say it. Please." Kenzie allowed him to continue. His leg was no longer shaking, and he felt strong enough to stand up. Kenzie followed him and rose to her feet as well. "I sort of feel like I'm on top of the world up here, you know? Like I can do anything I want without analyzing or second guessing. I'm free from it all." Kenzie watched him take a few steps away from her and he stumbled slightly but quickly caught himself. Kenzie had to catch her breath. Yes, he was a clumsy guy even before the diagnosis that would little by little rob him of all muscle coordination. But this was hard to watch. Any stumble, even if it was not related to Peter's illness, now made Kenzie panic and react in an attempt to steady him every time. She remained still this time as she watched him back up to the far rail, again leaning up against it.

"What are you second guessing?" Kenzie asked, hoping for a brief, insecure moment that it wasn't marrying her.

"My need to put you through the time I have left, for my own comfort," Peter admitted. "Is that selfish?"

Kenzie looked at him for a long moment. There was a silent stare between them until she expressed exactly how she felt about what he had just asked her. "Selfish? *You* feel selfish? How do you think *I* feel? Here I am married to the man of my dreams. God gave me you, but not without a ticking time bomb attached. In just a matter of months my life is going to explode, and you will be gone and I will be alone. I pray to God every time there is silence in my head – all day and all night long. And do you know what I'm asking of him? No, not asking, that's the wrong word. It's more like pleading. I want and I need for you to live. I don't ask God to help you die quickly and painlessly because to suffer is not what you deserve. Instead, I repeatedly have prayed for God to keep you here with me. To grant us a miracle. I'm thinking of myself, I'm dreading that moment when you close your eyes for that final time. I don't want to feel lost and alone. So, who's being selfish now?" There were tears rolling off of Kenzie's face, as her voice remained calm and clear, but there was overwhelming pain manifested in her eyes and facial expression.

"This is exactly what I mean," Peter spoke, keeping his distance from her with his body pressing harder against the railing. "I have put you here. I insisted we get married, take this honeymoon, and live the last of my days together. But look… look at what I am dragging you through. We have tried to live every moment and make the most of our time left together, but behind the smiles, the laughter, and feeling so high on love, we are both barely hanging on here and it's slowly killing us. I'm dying anyway so for me it doesn't matter. But, for you, you damn well better believe it matters. When I met you, you were a strong, independent woman. I don't want to be the person who changes that, who steals that from you. I can't bring you down so far and then leave you to claw your way back up alone." Peter turned around, gripped the railing in front of him with both of his hands. He looked over and down, way down below, at the water. He knew they were at least eighty feet up. Just below the surface of the clear water, he could see very large rocks. That water below didn't contain any fish near the surface, or turtles, or the same octopus they spotted and were fascinated by on their climb earlier. The water was rushing over those rocks in a reckless manner. The rip current at the tip of the back side of Black Rock was fiercely strong today. And the conditions down there were dangerous.

Kenzie hurried over to him. Right by his side was where she wanted to be. "Stop talking crazy, Peter Sterling. You are not bringing me down. I love you with everything I am, and I will kick and scream and fight you like no one else ever has if you think you are going to push me away now. I need to be with you just as much as you need me by your side. Maybe more."

Peter reached for her hand, and she took it and held it tightly. He was no longer peering down at the water. He was looking at her. "Jump with me," was all she heard him say.

Chapter 4

Kenzie clung tighter to him. She held on for dear life. "What did you just say?"

"I would not have to deteriorate at the hands of this disease. You would not have to face life without me. I can't stand the thought of you with someone else, having children. Moving on." It was an admission that Peter should have been ashamed of, but it really only humanized him. He accepted it, and Kenzie understood it.

"You've watched Thelma and Louise too many times," Kenzie stated, feeling nervous and desperately trying to find the humor in something too crazy to comprehend.

"Not the same story at all. The police were after them. Fate is after me. Us, really," Peter tried to explain. "Go with me. Let's see together what's next. They say there is a hereafter where there is no pain, no sickness, or sadness. Let's find our happily ever after in paradise together."

"You are serious!" Kenzie raised her voice, widened her eyes, and continued to hold his hand and she stayed very close to him. If he was thinking about going over that railing, she had to do everything she could to stop him. Especially listen to his reasoning behind both of them giving up on life. She stood there and her mind flashed to her parents. They were in their late fifties, and not much had changed. The two of them were still very much into each other, and hardly cared if Kenzie called or visited. For a moment, Kenzie was back to her childhood, at five years old, sitting at the dinner table eating fancy food, feeling unloved and ignored. If she believed her parents needed her or cared if her life ended today, she would be lying to herself. But, she did have love in her life, outside of her relationship with her husband. She's always had Gi and Lizzy. Their bond was indestructible. Their friendship had been life-long. They loved each other unconditionally. Soul sisters in every sense. She was thinking of them now. She had not been honest with them about this current crisis in her life because Peter needed her to keep his secret. But, because she could not confide in her friends, she was feeling lost. If she had given them the chance to support her and just love her through this pain, maybe she would have more courage to face what was happening. It wouldn't hurt any less, but they could still be there for her. Thinking of Gi and

Lizzy right now was what pulled Kenzie back to reality. *This wasn't her time. Nor was it Peter's.* Not yet.

"Kenz... I'm not strong enough to endure it. I'm a third generation man who is going to lose his dignity and then die. I have the power to stop that. To end it now. With you. Let's hold our breaths and jump. And when we open our eyes again, we'll be together for eternity." Peter was trying his damndest to convince his wife that this sudden justification made sense.

"Was this your plan all along? Coming to Hawaii? Climbing this cliff with me?" Kenzie tried hard to keep her voice calm.

"No, honestly, it wasn't," Peter was quick to answer. "It's just being up here. I told you, I feel free. I think what I'm most afraid of right now is losing you."

"Killing ourselves isn't the answer. It shouldn't even be crossing your mind," Kenzie tried to convince him.

"You're not the one dying!" he snapped at her.

"No, I'm not. But, I am losing my greatest reason for living." Kenzie meant that. She did, however, force herself to think of Gi and Lizzy again. They were her family, too.

"You say things like that and I believe you understand. You get why we should do this. But then you pull back. Why?" She could see the pain in Peter's eyes. She had disappointed him.

"Because I see us eventually moving away from this railing and making our way down that cliff. I imagine us making love in our hotel room many more times before this trip ends and we go home together to face what's next. One day at a time. Peter, we cannot react to how we feel in one crazy impulsive moment. I see us with more time. And I want that." As she finished speaking, Kenzie took a hold of his other hand. She was now gripping both of his hands tightly with hers. Her feet were firmly planted on the ground as she stepped away from the railing. While Peter was still much stronger than her, Kenzie managed to pull him toward her, and just a few feet away from the railing. He willingly followed her.

"You are not inside of my body, and you do not know what kind of thinking goes on in my mind. It gets pretty desperate," Peter told her.

"I gather that now," she teased him and smiled.

"Take me down the side of the cliff before I lose my marbles up here again," Peter sighed, and Kenzie let go of his hands as she leaned into him and they kissed. It was a kiss that made them both feel loved. And happy to be alive.

Their lips parted and they began to walk away with their arms around each other. "Ah, wait, the backpack," Peter stopped her.

"I'll get it," Kenzie offered, but Peter moved first just as he said, "No, let me."

The backpack was on the ground just below the bottom railing. There were two rails protecting the hikers from the cliff. One reached Peter's chest and the lower one met his knees. When Peter bent forward to retrieve the orange backpack, he took a hold of one of the straps and had unknowingly been standing on the opposite strap hanging loose and partly touching the ground. He tugged upward on the backpack and when it wouldn't budge that motion instantly jerked his entire body forward. His reflexes were weak. The space between the top and bottom railing was adequate room for an adult's body to fit through. And it happened entirely too quickly for a man who made a clumsy move to catch himself. Or for his wife to save him from that deadly high fall into the shallow water with too many large rocks and a dangerous current.

Chapter 5

Twenty-four hours later, Gi was working at her store, located in downtown Dogpatch, which was the prime gift shopping area for tourists. She had just checked out one customer and a half a dozen others were browsing when the glass door to Gi's Gems wildly swung open and the chime on the door did a frenzied double ding. Gi immediately looked up and saw Lizzy barreling inside.

She kept her voice low when Lizzy reached her, where only a counter separated them. "I know I told you to stop by anytime, but I'll need a few minutes before I can give you my full attention. It's pretty hectic in here right now. It's been like this all day actually. Not enough coffee and middle fingers to get through the day!" Gi giggled at her own statement, still purposely trying to keep her voice low, but Lizzy didn't react to another typical snarky comment of hers.

"You haven't checked your phone, have you?" Lizzy asked her.

"No, who has time for that? I've been busy!" Gi reminded her again, and this time she felt frustrated.

"Something happened in Hawaii. Kenzie needs us to meet her at the airport. She's flying out of Maui at midnight and into Columbia Regional around eight tomorrow morning." Lizzy appeared calm because there were customers present, but Gi had known better. She knew all too well that Lizzy was nervous.

"What the hell happened?" Gi asked.

"I don't know. Kenzie's text was so vague that it's both irritating and scaring me! She just wants us to meet her at the airport. She said please. She said something awful happened. She's not returning my texts or calls and quite frankly I am freaking out." Lizzy needed to take a breath, and Gi wanted to get her customers out of the store so she could possibly close it down early, or at least find the time to make her own attempt to reach Kenzie. Gi had always been the type of person who needed to know what she was walking into in any given situation. If that were possible.

Gi and Kenzie were sixty minutes early, sitting side by side on a row of six chairs at the airport's main gate. In one hour, they would have answers from Kenzie. "I know I've said this too many times since yesterday, but it really pisses me off that Kenz will not reply to either of us," Gi said, checking the phone in her hand one more time for missed messages.

"You know how she is…when something bad happens, she shuts down," Lizzy stated. "At least she reached out to us, and she will tell us when she's ready. Something tells me Kenzie is really going to need us this time. One minute we married her off, the next she was on an amazing honeymoon. And now, we assume, she's on her way home alone? What in the world could have happened?"

"Maybe Peter told her he's gay?" Gi cracked a smile as Lizzy shook her head.

"Were you not listening at all when she described the kind of sex life they have?" Lizzy remarked. "Geez, half of that I had to Google."

Gi laughed out loud, and then said, "You sure are missing out," but after she spoke those words, she wanted to take them back. What she saw a couple of days ago in the front yard of Lizzy's house seriously made her wonder if Lizzy was teetering on the brink of cheating on her husband.

"I don't like it when you say that to me," Lizzy admitted. "But, it's true though. I've never had a relationship with fire. I seriously hate sex and could do without it in my life."

"I'm sorry," Gi said, patting her leg overtop her dark washed capri denim. "Sex can really be something if it's done right. But, you know, it's not just about two physical bodies finding pleasure. Your heart, your head, it's all gotta be in it one hundred and ten percent. And to be honest, Liz, it's been a very long time since I've even wanted to be that close to Ric."

Lizzy nodded her head, because she knew. Even though Gi preferred to pretend she was happy with her life, her closest friends saw the signs of unhappiness. But, for Lizzy, she never really felt unhappy. She was content to be settled into her life with Max and Griffin. "Marriage is strange, and it's definitely not the same for everyone. We do what we have to do, or what we become accustomed to doing. But I was really hoping it would be different for Kenzie." Gi agreed as Lizzy spoke.

"It can still be. We have no idea what happened, and while we wait, I want to hear more about Hank the Hunk," Gi pressed her.

"Should we really get into that here?" Lizzy asked her. She still had not reached the point of completely admitting her growing feelings of infatuation for another man to herself yet.

"Yes. Spill it," Gi ordered her.

"We are friends, I guess. I enjoy talking to him. We do flirt when we see each other. And there have been times when I've gone to Plant Land just to see him," Lizzy looked down at her feet on the floor before she continued because she felt a little ashamed to be saying it out loud. "It didn't start out that way, but this feeling is different for me. I like it. I find myself daydreaming about him. I love my husband and all he's done for me and my son, our son," Lizzy was quick to correct herself.

"But you wonder at twenty-eight years old if there's more out there for you? Is there a life –and are there feelings– that you have not experienced yet, and could?" Gi was a master at this. She, too, wondered the same, but had held on and stayed committed to her marriage for her little girl.

"Yes. Oh my gosh, yes," Lizzy replied. "How terrible of a person am I? Max gave me everything. And he loves me and Griffin with all that he is."

"He's a good man, Lizzie," Gi told her. "And I want to set your ass straight, and tell you to stop this right now. But I don't know if I can. A part of me wants you to run to this new man and have him literally take you like you've never experienced. But cheating is not something you can just check off your list and then resume your marriage and your life as you know it, like nothing happened. There are consequences. Or, you may not be able to get him out of your system, and do you really even know how he feels? Maybe he's only looking to get naked."

"I'm going to start by telling you that I don't want to cheat on Max. That's not me. Or is it? Has my mundane life led me to want to be someone different? Maybe to be more of a risk taker?" Lizzy questioned herself. "And, really, if Hank was only after sex, he could choose any woman, a much less chunky one for sure."

"You're beautiful, Lizzy. You know that." Gi always reminded her of that. "So what if the number on the scale is higher than you'd like it to be. You are the best version of yourself -kind, loving, giving, strong in your faith- and to me that's pretty damn perfect. *You* are pretty damn perfect."

"I love you for getting life the way you do," Lizzy told Gi as their hands met.

"I dwell a lot. That's how I figure shit out," Gi teased and they both laughed. Before they could resume their conversation about Lizzy's budding inappropriate feelings, another woman twice their age walked up and sat down near them, only leaving one empty chair between her and Gi.

"Hello ladies," she greeted them, and Gi and Lizzy both said *hello* to her. "I guess you've heard about the accident in Hawaii?" the woman asked, pointing up to the television, now on CNN, and the news reporter was on location near what looked like a wall of a cliff near the ocean. At the moment it was difficult to hear the television and listen to the woman speak, so Gi immediately stood up and walked closer to the televised live broadcast, hoping to hear better. "Don't bother," the woman stopped her. "The news isn't giving too much information yet. My daughter was in Maui, she's on the flight home now. She called me about the tragedy." It was a tossup whose eyes were wider -Gi's or Lizzy's- as Gi walked back toward her seat.

Neither one spoke a word. They were both afraid to. They just waited for the woman to continue on. "A man apparently fell to his death. That cliff jumping has become more and more dangerous. My daughter is obsessed with it, but now maybe after what happened to that young man in water too shallow and a current too dangerous, she will think twice."

"A young man?" Gi finally spoke, and Lizzy swallowed hard. "Do you have a name?"

"I'm not sure if one has been released yet, you know how the family all must be notified first," the woman stated. "At first the news was saying it was a freak accident, then something was mentioned about suicide. My daughter said she heard both on the beach as well." The woman continued to speak and with every word out of her mouth, Gi and Lizzy grew more nervous. Suicide, they both knew, was out of the question for their best friend's brand new husband. But, an accident occurring when two very adventurous people were on their honeymoon was entirely probable.

They already knew something bad had happened, but the thought of Kenzie returning from her honeymoon a widow had suddenly forced an unimaginable fear to surface in both of them. And now the passengers from the flight Kenzie was supposed to be on were filing into the airport.

*

At least five minutes had passed as Gi and Lizzy scanned every face that walked by. There was still no sign of Kenzie. Neither one of them had gotten up. They continued to sit beside each other, shoulders touching, in silence. And finally they both saw her.

Her long blonde hair was in a messy knot, perched high on top of her head. She never wore her prescription glasses, only contacts, but she was wearing those dark-wire rims today. A sleeveless heather gray dress nearly reached her ankles where she wore a plain pair of black flip flops on her feet. To anyone walking by, Kenzie looked like a model, even sans makeup on the long flight. But, to her friends, she was just Kenz. And, right now, they saw pain in her eyes and the expression she wore told them both to get to her fast. *Run.*

The three women abruptly met in a huddle, off to the side of the crowd. While holding each other tightly, both Gi and Lizzy heard Kenzie crying. Her muffled cry intensely turned into a deep, gut-wrenching sob.

Gi was always the first to speak. They stayed close in their huddle, but pulled back to see each other's faces. "Tell us what happened to him," she began.

"Here?" Lizzy asked, always being the one to worry about privacy.

"Yes, here!" Gi snapped, only thinking of Kenzie and how much she needed them. Right now. She had been alone and keeping something to herself long enough.

Kenzie moved her body up against a nearby wall. She plopped her carry-on luggage down on the floor near her feet. "My husband is dead," she spoke clearly, and her words forced more tears onto her already tear-soaked face. Lizzy covered her own mouth with her hand, and Gi momentarily closed her own eyes. "We were hiking the side of a cliff and he ended up plunging into water that was just too dangerous for him to survive." There was more to the story, so much more, but those details needed to wait while her friends did their best to comfort her. Against a random wall in an airport that wasn't too overly crowded early in the morning, the three of them cried for the loss of a really good man. They had all loved him. But it was Kenzie who was going to be lost without him.

✱

"I can't cry anymore," Kenzie told them, as a few more tears unwillingly seeped out of her eyes and rolled down her flushed cheeks.

The three of them were perched on high stools around a small round table in the airport's bar. Kenzie had said she needed a drink, and no one second guessed her. They each were drinking a Bloody Mary at five minutes past nine in the morning.

"Okay, I'm ready," Kenzie said, touching her manicured red fingernails to the condensation on her glass. Her drink was half gone, and she had taken a few deep breaths before speaking. "You're both going to be shocked, and you will have five thousand questions, but please just hear me out. Let me speak of the entire story before you say anything." Both Gi and Lizzy nodded their heads, and waited.

"Peter only had six months to live. I knew that when I married him. He was the third generation male in his family to be diagnosed with Huntington's. You both know the story of his father and grandfather." Kenzie paused, and it took everything in Gi not to speak. To blurt out a curse word felt essential at the moment. But, she remained quiet. And Lizzy again had covered her mouth with her hand, which was always a gesture she made when she was shocked or moved to tears. "We wanted so badly to get married, to experience a honeymoon, and just live out the rest of his months together. But, Peter was struggling with the changes his body was already going through, and especially with the fear of what he knew was ahead."

"For fuck's sake! He jumped to his death on purpose!" Gi couldn't help herself. Lizzy instantly gave her a look of disapproval.

Kenzie responded, "Shut up, Gi. Can you not respect what I just asked of you?"

"I'm sorry," Gi regretfully spoke, and Kenzie continued to fill in the blanks.

"Did Peter kill himself on our honeymoon? No," Kenzie stated. "But he wanted to. We hiked the side of Black Rock and we stopped and talked for a long while. He swore to me that he had not preplanned anything. It was just how he was feeling up there. Free. And wanting to end it all before he had to endure the craziness of the disease – and put me through it, too. He really did love me so very much."

Kenzie took a long drink from her Bloody Mary, wishing the bartender would have doubled the vodka in it. "He had a moment of desperation up there, and he tried to talk me into jumping with him. He wanted us to be together now and forever," Kenzie sighed. "I don't want either of you to ever judge him for that. Or me, for that matter."

"Are you saying you considered doing it?" This time Lizzy interrupted.

"It's your turn to shut up," Gi immediately directed her comment at Lizzy, and Kenzie smiled softly. *Those were her girls.*

"Okay, so maybe expecting you both to just listen to this incomprehensible story was too much to ask. But, I'm not done speaking yet…" Kenzie continued. "Up there, on top of the world, I thought about how Peter is my life. My parents are useless to me. My career doesn't mean as much to me anymore. And then my thoughts circled around the two of you. My friends who are my soul sisters. Trinity in every sense of the word. I need the two of you so much. I couldn't bear the thought of leaving you both." By now the three of them were holding hands in the middle of the table just like they had done for the very first time nearly three decades ago in kindergarten. "This pain is too intense and so terribly raw. I need you both to help me deal with it, or I'll never be the same."

"Of course we will, honey, but you are never going to be the same regardless," Lizzy told her in the most comforting way. "There is no way around the pain…you have to go into it, through it, and you have to push and shove to get to the other side of it. The world you find there will never be the same as the world you left."

Kenzie knew Lizzy was greatly affected by the people around her who didn't know how to handle grief. When her mother died, she grew up watching her father ignore the pain and her mother's memory. "I need your wisdom from your own awful experience," Kenzie begged Lizzy, "And, Gi, I need your strength, that powerful force you embody when you need to plow through life's pain."

"You have us and all we have to offer," Gi spoke, brushing the hair out of her eyes, and both Lizzy and Kenzie saw the tears pooling in them.

"He didn't jump," Kenzie stated, defending her husband's memory. "He realized why he shouldn't after I told him I wouldn't join him, or allow him to leave me like that. He had a moment of weakness and desperation, and it all obviously stemmed from fear."

"Then how did it happen? How did he fall? How did he die?" Gi wanted so badly to understand this, as did Lizzy.

"Remember the time you called him trippy?" Kenzie asked Gi.

"Oh my God," Lizzy stated, as Gi couldn't speak and only shook her head.

"He went back for our backpack. It was near the railing. He was a clumsy guy, but his illness had really taken a toll on his reflexes lately. The strap was tangled, he jerked the bag, and his body went over. God, it happened so terribly fast. There was nothing I could do. I never had a chance to move, to help him." Kenzie choked on a sob and both Gi and Lizzy stood up, walked to her, and immediately enveloped her into their arms.

It was like a funeral. The hugs, the tears, the moments of strength, and the times when nothing held them back from falling apart. Because that's what they wanted –and needed– to do.

When Kenzie felt stronger again, the other two sat back down on their stools near her.

"They found his body. I don't want to describe how helpless and scared out of my mind I felt having to hang over that railing and watch what happened to him. Or, how I could not get down from the trail on the side of that cliff fast enough to the beach. He hit the rocks in the water, and then the rip current took him under. I waited for them, the recovery team, to bring him to me, so I could say goodbye. I couldn't take that kind of pain, and I needed to get out of there. I wasted no time, and insisted on cremation. There wasn't a need for an autopsy. I know he was sick. I know how he fell. He didn't jump. I couldn't bear the thought of coming back home with his body on that plane. I scattered his ashes on the beach before I left. But now I don't even know if he would have approved of being cremated."

"Stop, Kenz," Gi spoke up. "You did what you needed to do. And, one day, when you are ready, Liz and I will go back there with you. We will sit in the sand on that beach and feel close to Peter together. He would approve of that."

Chapter 6

When Gi walked into her house, she found Suzie sitting on the floor in front of the television. She had a bowl of Spaghetti O's on her lap with a spoon sunk in it. It was dinner time. Gi had texted Ric and told him to feed their daughter, because she had been unsure of what time she would be home. Right now, Ric wasn't in the room and Gi suddenly flashed back to the days when she was a child eating dinner alone every night in front of the television.

"Hey baby girl," Gi caught her daughter's attention.

"Mommy! Daddy said you had to work at the store late. I don't know why you didn't pick me up from school and bring me there with you like you always do." Suzie had turned her back to the television while she spoke to her mother. She was wearing all pale pink colors. Her shorts. Her shirt. And her high top tennis shoes with the laces untied. Her auburn hair looked messy from a long day at school, or probably from hard play at recess.

"I had something very important to do, but I'm here now," Gi told her. "Where is your daddy?"

"He got a tow call," Suzie stated, and Gi's eyes widened. Ric owned and operated a towing service in Lake Ozark, eight miles from where they lived.

"Why didn't he take you along with him?" Gi inhaled a slow, steady breath through her nostrils. That was her attempt at trying to keep calm.

"Because my dinner was ready from the microwave and I wanted to stay here and eat it."

"Sooz, you're five. You shouldn't be home alone. Next time, please go with daddy." At this point, Gi was so angry she couldn't fathom *a next time*. As a husband, Ric had run out of second chances a long time ago. But Gi never before had questioned his ability to be a good father.

Before Suzie could finish chewing and swallowing a heaping spoonful of Spaghetti O's and respond that her daddy said he would be right back, the door opened and in walked Ric.

"Hey, you're back," he said, looking as if he had lost the race to get home first.

"You left her here alone?" Gi never messed around with small talk. She said what she was thinking as soon as any thought entered her brain. Right now, however, she was trying not to scream in front of her child. And she was about to fail at it.

"I got a call for a tow, just a few miles away. It's all good. Sooz is a big girl. She's fine," Ric pointed at her sitting on the floor in front of the TV as if Gi needed to take another look at their daughter to see for herself.

"I know she's fine," Gi spoke through clenched teeth. "Can I talk to you about this in the kitchen?" Gi stormed past him and he reluctantly followed her.

She stood against the countertop with her arms folded across her chest. He walked into the kitchen in faded denim, a navy blue fitted t-shirt, and still wearing his ankle-high brown work boots. Through the kitchen window, Gi had already seen the tow truck with an attached car parked along the curb. Gi knew Ric had not driven the eight miles all the way back to his shop. He had gone to rescue a customer a few miles away and came right back. Still, he wasn't excused. He never should have left their little girl at home by herself.

"Look, I know you're mad. I'm sorry. It was stupid. I won't do it again, I swear." Ric rarely apologized. It just wasn't his nature. Gi wondered if he understood that their marriage had been long over, but their family was still intact because of that little girl sitting in the other room. If Ric screwed up with her, that would be it for Gi.

Gi was tough. She rarely let anyone see her fall apart. But at this moment, after the day she had, she lost control and broke down. She brought both of her hands to her face and just held her head and sobbed.

At first, Ric was completely taken aback. The wife he was accustomed to would have screamed at him and held her own with every single curse word. He felt pained believing he was the root of her breakdown right now, but he didn't understand her reaction.

Ric walked over to his wife and reached for both of her shoulders. "Hey…are you okay? Jesus. You're making me feel like shit. I told you, I know I'm a stupid ass. I will take her along next time, no matter how mad she gets about the Spaghetti O's being hot and ready to eat."

"Did you ever think about taking the bowl of noodles along?" Gi spoke, and attempted to smile through her tears. She knew Suzie was a force to be reckoned with. And she was well aware of how Ric so easily caved for her.

"No, but next time!" Ric stated, and Gi did smile at him then. He was so boyish and he could be a charmer. For a brief moment, she remembered what it felt like to love him.

But her verbal response was altogether the opposite of her mixed feelings right now. "I'm mad at you, don't think I'm not. I seriously will think twice about leaving her with you next time. But, I can't deal with you right now," Gi told him, as she wiped another tear from her cheek.

"What happened to you today? You never said where you were." Ric suddenly felt worried. She didn't look like herself at all. If someone had hurt his wife in any way, he would kill them with his bare hands. He used to express his concern about her being in the store alone. *You never know about any stranger who walked in off the street.* Gi was independent and strong, but she was a woman Ric used to feel very protective of. Somehow that feeling was lost along the way, too.

"Lizzy and I picked up Kenz at the airport. She flew all night long from Hawaii." Gi sighed, because she knew she had to tell Ric what happened. He was actually the first person she would say the words aloud to. And that just made this tragedy all the more real.

"So she and Peter needed a ride home? Why didn't they leave a car at the airport like everyone else does?" Ric asked.

"Peter didn't come back with her," Gi managed to say.

"She left him in Hawaii? What the hell? Are they at odds already? You and I made it longer than that before we started–" he was going to say *throwing insults,* or *growing apart,* but he didn't like how either sounded, so he just stopped talking in mid sentence.

"There was an accident, and Peter died." Gi looked down at the linoleum floor in the kitchen. It needed to be replaced. The older home they were excited about refurbishing five years ago still needed many more upgrades. It was as if that house mirrored their marriage. They had both given up on it, too, but continued to live in it and walk all over it.

"Oh Christ! You've got to be kidding me? What kind of accident?" Ric ran his fingers through his hair and shook his head.

"He fell off of a cliff, they were hiking, and he lost his balance," Gi spit the words out clearly and quickly. "But, that's not all..." she continued. "Peter could be clumsy. We all know that and we've all cracked a joke about it. He also was sick. He had HD like the rest of the men in his family. It was slowly destroying his muscle coordination."

"That's terrible, I don't know what else to say. Makes me sick, really. How's Kenzie?" The man standing before her right now was not the man Gi had grown to hate over time. This was the Ric Sutter she used to be able to talk to, and love.

"Not good," Gi replied, trying not to notice how sensitive and caring he was being. She didn't want to be sucked into that once more with him – only to be let down and hurt again.

"I can watch Suzie if you need to go back to her tonight," Ric offered, and Gi shot him a disapproving look before she responded.

"I'm still very pissed off at you for being irresponsible with her," she told him in no uncertain terms.

"Then I'm outta here until you cool off," he told her. "I'll be at the shop if anything changes with you." He turned on his heels and walked out the kitchen door. And just like that, the old Ric was back.

At that moment, Gi wondered what she would have given for him to comfort her. To take her in his arms, or kiss her on the forehead, as he had done so many times in the past. But then, she reminded herself that those old feelings were too far gone.

Chapter 7

When Lizzy got home, both Max and Griffin met her at the front door as she stepped inside.

"Mom! We just saw the news! They said Peter died in Hawaii?" The media had released his name. Griffin's face wore the same kind of shock they all were feeling. *It just couldn't be true.*

"It's true, Grif," Lizzy's voice cracked and Max immediately stepped closer to her and pulled her into hug. That big, burly man sure knew how to be tender. She heard him say *how sorry he was for her pain and Kenzie's pain and then he asked her how it happened. The news had said it was a cliff jumping accident.*

"They were hiking, not jumping," Lizzy began to explain. "It's a sad story, really, just as sad as it is shocking. Peter was sick. No one knew but him and Kenz. He was dying of the same disease that took the lives of his father and grandfather. It's called Huntington's and it can affect muscle coordination. Peter stumbled and fell to his death. The water was rocky and the current was too strong." Lizzy stopped talking. All of this was just too much right now. Max pulled her into his arms again and held her close. He rubbed her back while she cried. When she was in her husband's embrace, she noticed Griffin slipped out of the room with tears in his eyes.

"Thank you, Max," she said, backing out of his arms.

"Sure," he replied, "is there anything you need? Are you helping Kenzie with the arrangements?"

"Unless Kenzie changes her mind, there will be no funeral or memorial," Lizzy told him. "Peter was cremated and Kenzie already scattered his ashes on the beach in Maui, in close proximity to where he died."

"Seems sudden and not well thought out," Max offered his opinion a little too lightly, even though he knew the law in most states was twenty-four hours following death, a body could be cremated. Lizzy immediately jumped to the defense of her best friend.

"Kenzie did what she thought was best. It's really hard to think when your husband dies on your honeymoon. I mean, come on, anyone who has a heart wouldn't judge her for spreading his ashes there. He loved the ocean and the sand."

Max only nodded his head. He knew his wife was emotional, and she had every right to be. He also knew that besides their son, those two women in her life were her entire world. He never could compete with them, but he certainly tried. *Tomorrow, or the following day, he would buy his wife a new vehicle. The SUV she currently drove was already a year old. She deserved a new one. It would make her feel better. And would remind her how much her husband loved her.*

"I'm going upstairs to take a bubble bath," Lizzy stated. I just want to soak this sadness away."

"I'll make dinner," Max called after her, and Lizzy only replied a faint *okay* as she was already walking up the stairway.

Lizzy had noticed Griffin's bedroom door was closed, and she respected his need for space. She walked into the master bathroom. When she stepped in there, she dropped her capri jeans to the floor, and then unbuttoned her three-quarter length blouse. Before she took off her shirt, she heard her cell phone beep. It was still in the pocket of her pants, now on the floor. She bent down and retrieved it.

And then she read the text. From Hank Stewart.

I heard the awful news. I remember from high school how close you, Gi and Kenzie always were. I want to offer my deepest condolences, a listening ear, or my shoulder to cry on. Anytime.

Lizzy looked at herself in the mirror. She still felt unbearably sad, but the message from Hank had thrown her a rope. Something to hold onto and begin to pull herself up with. The mere thought of where that rope led felt new but comfortable, and also quite intriguing.

She bent down to pick up her pants off the floor. She stepped back into them, and sucked in her stomach a bit to fasten the button and zipper again. She checked closely in the mirror to see if her mascara had run underneath her eyes. She combed through her hair for a moment, and then she left the bathroom. After she slipped into her sandals by the bed, she descended the stairs. When she reached the doorway of the kitchen, she saw Max with the refrigerator door open and two pots and pans were setting on the stovetop.

"I'm going to Kenz. She needs me for awhile." Lizzy was already out of the front door when it occurred to her. That was the first lie she had ever told him. She never before in their marriage had a reason to lie. Or to keep a secret.

✱

While she drove, she responded to Hank's text. *Thank you. I may take you up on your offer to talk. Are you at Plant Land right now?*

His response was an immediate *Yes.*

Lizzy set her phone down in the cup holder between the seats, and she focused on driving. She told herself not to over think this one. To just go with what she wanted. She didn't need to be reminded that life was fleeting and entirely too short. She learned that in the worst way as a little girl when she lost her mother. Kenzie's loss, however, brought all of those feelings to the surface again. Lizzy was devastated for her best friend, and the way Hank reached out to her had instantly affected her.

She drove onto the empty parking lot at Plant Land. It was after closing time, but she saw light in the building and Hank's truck was parked out front. And when she got out of her vehicle and walked up to the main entrance, Hank was on the other side of that glass door. And he opened it for her.

"Hi there," he spoke first. "You look like you could use a friend."

"You couldn't be more right," she replied, softly smiling at him. Only he was wrong about her needing a friend. Lizzy had two of the best friends in her life already. She didn't need friends. She needed Hank. And whatever he had to offer her right now, Lizzy wanted. Second guessing and analyzing were not going to be allowed to enter her mind tonight.

"Come sit down in my office," he offered as they walked on the concrete floor through the entire store. It felt strange to be in there while it was closed for business, but Lizzy just kept moving with him.

When they reached Hank's office, he again offered her a seat. Lizzy sat down on the small black leather sofa against the wall. "Fancy furniture for a store office?" she commented and Hank laughed out loud. "It's actually a love seat that I didn't have room for in my apartment with the sofa. My ex-wife didn't want the set."

"I see," Lizzy spoke, feeling comfortable where she was sitting, but tense about what she was doing. But, as soon as those apprehensive thoughts entered her mind, she pushed them out.

"Do you want to talk about it?" Hank asked her, referring to the accident.

"Not really. The news coverage pretty much summed it up. It doesn't matter how it happened, what matters is my best friend needs me and I will be there for her." Lizzy felt teary thinking of it all again.

"Of course you will," Hank told her. "And I'm here for you. I mean, if you want to have a drink or talk about anything."

"Should a married woman be having a drink with a single man?" Lizzy surprised herself when she asked him that.

"You're here, aren't you?" he asked her rather bluntly.

"I am," she said, as she watched him sit down beside her. The cushions were close together and so were they.

"There's something between us," Hank admitted, turning his body sideways to face her.

"I've really tried not to recognize it…" Lizzy said, looking at him and then looking down at her hands folded together on her lap.

"We can be friends if that is only what you want," Hank told her, as he placed his thumb and forefinger on her chin and gently forced her to look up at him.

"Friends. Yes. I enjoy your company," she said, feeling awkward and foolish for coming there.

"Elizabeth?" he said her name as if he wanted to ask her something. She looked at him, feeling nervous and her heart was pounding so fast she could hear it in her ears. "I want to kiss you so badly, but I won't if you tell me not to. I know how to respect a marriage. It's just that when I'm with you, I don't care what is right or wrong." Hank's hands were on his lap now, and Lizzy reached for one. He was so masculine. His hand was huge, and both calloused and soft in places. She intertwined her fingers with his. And then she brought his fingers up to her lips as they both turned toward each other.

He moved his hand further on her neck and downward to her collarbone. She wanted to close her eyes and savor that feeling. His touch had instantly taken her somewhere else. Somewhere forbidden.

"Hank, I want this, I do," Lizzy started to say to him.

"But?" he asked her, already assuming what she would say next.

"But I can't. I shouldn't be here." Lizzy's conscious was finally back.

When Hank stopped touching her, Lizzy stood up. He followed her to his feet. "I understand," he stated, believing she was about to walk away from what he thought she wanted as much as he did.

"Would you understand if I asked you to kiss me and then let me walk out that door?" Lizzy spoke freely and honestly to him without uncertainties. "I am so embarrassed to say this, but the first boy I ever kissed when I was sixteen years old, I slept with. The next man I gave my body to, I married. I don't know how to take it slow. I don't know how to make out with a man and not take it all the way. Show me how, Hank…"

Hank smiled at her. There was still such innocence about her that he recognized, and had fallen for, the moment he met her. He took both of his hands and placed them on her face. He was at least three inches taller than her, so he came down to meet her lips with his. He kissed her slowly and tenderly. It was a few moments before their tongues met. And for the first time in her life, Lizzy felt that fire everyone talked about. His kisses were deep and passionate and literally breathtaking. They kissed endlessly before their hands started to roam on each other's bodies. He fondled her breasts through her buttoned blouse. She had her hands on his hard chest overtop his white t-shirt. Both of his hands went to her rear. Her fingers traced the bulge in the front of his jeans. And when he groaned, she backed away.

"Just kissing? Are you sure?" he asked, almost whining.

"Push me out that door," she begged him.

"I would like to push you up against it and take you right here." Hank's voice was raspy.

"Next time," she said, as she kissed him hard on the mouth, thrusting her tongue against his. And then she rushed out of his office without looking back. Because, if she had looked back at him, she would have so effortlessly ran to him, fallen back into his arms and deeper into this feeling she had found with another man.

The car behind her at the red light honked twice. Lizzy quickly came to her senses, lifted her foot off of the brake and pressed down hard on the gas pedal. *Sometimes she could get completely caught up in those daydreams.*

Chapter 8

Staring straight ahead in the dark, Kenzie sat on the sofa in the condo she shared with Peter, months before they were married. She had insisted Gi and Lizzy go home. They had their families to tend to. *Their husbands were waiting.* That was such a lonely thought now, knowing she no longer had anyone waiting for her. While Kenzie was the last of the three of them to fall in love for keeps and to marry, she had believed finding Peter was worth the wait. And now it was beyond unfair that he was already taken away from her. *Did Lizzy really love Max, or did she love the life he provided for her? And what about Gi – she spends so much time fighting with Ric!* Kenzie knew it was wrong to compare and to believe she was most deserving to keep her husband because she and Peter were more in love than anyone else. She just felt selfish right now, and that was warranted, as she was sinking lower into her grief.

She uncurled her body on the sofa and reached forward onto the coffee table for both a wine bottle and a stemless glass. She poured herself another drink, finishing off what was left in the bottle. With her glass in hand, she curled her legs back up on the sofa, and sank into the pillows around her. She took a generous swig from her glass and momentarily closed her eyes, and that's all it took for the tears already pooling in them to spill over onto her cheeks. *Missing Peter and their life together hurt so badly.*

Kenzie didn't know how long she had dozed off, but she was startled awake when her doorbell rang. The house was still completely dark. The sun had long set through the open blinds of the many large windows in her condo. She wasn't in any mood for visitors. Her brief time spent today with Peter's parents had drained her, precisely because they were upset about her refusal to have a funeral or at least a memorial service for their son. Kenzie had definitely felt reprimanded for having Peter cremated so quickly and already scattering his ashes. She politely reminded them of how she was his wife, and entitled to do what she chose. Right now, she couldn't handle much more.

Still wearing her ankle-length sleeveless heather gray dress, Kenzie walked barefoot on the hardwood floors of her condo, toward the front door. She never asked who it was, nor had she peered out the window first. And when she opened the door, Lizzy was staring back at her.

"Liz, it's late. You should be at home with your family," Kenzie told her, as she stepped back from the door and Lizzy came inside and immediately hugged her.

"God, you always did give the best hugs," Kenzie muttered, tightening her arms around Lizzy.

"It's all the body fat," Lizzy teased as they parted. "A hug, or whatever you need from me, is why I came back. It just didn't feel right to be at home and know you were here alone."

"Come sit," Kenzie said, turning on a lamp in the living room as she walked in front of Lizzy in the dark.

After they sat close on the sofa, Kenzie picked up her empty stemless wine glass, placed between the cushions. "Can I get you a drink?"

"No," Lizzy replied, thinking Kenzie should resist another as well.

"It eases the pain," Kenzie defended her actions and Lizzie didn't disagree.

"That kind of pain is a bitch," Lizzy stated, as a matter of fact. "I still feel the cutting edges of it. Time will help you adjust to the idea of *this is how my life is now*, but the hurt never completely subsides."

"You kept a lot in when your mother died," Kenzie gathered, "but yet you managed to handle it in such a healthy way, didn't you?"

"Well, let's see," Lizzy began, "my father paved the way for Lance and I to move onward and upward. We didn't speak of her because he didn't. We all thought the other would be happier if my mother's memory wasn't brought up to consequently make us sad. Lance was too young to realize what was happening, but I wasn't. I thought I was dealing with losing my mother. I had you and Gi to talk about her with, and I visited her grave so much to communicate with her as if she was still with me. But, really, as I look back...I ended up pregnant at sixteen, I married a man who promised me the world at only eighteen, and now I'm twenty-eight years old and a part of me is just beginning to feel like an adult, finally a woman with her own opinion, and I want to reevaluate my life."

"I can see what you mean about how you may have spiraled with a few of the choices you've made, but that's you isn't it?" Kenzie reminded her. "You don't always look before you leap because in the moment of feeling safe, secure, and loved – you just trust it's all going to be okay. And, you know what? For you, eventually it has all turned out okay. It's not a bad way to live, Liz."

"No, it hasn't been. Until now," Lizzie replied. "When I initially left my house tonight, I was not on my way here. I lied to my husband and told him you needed me and this was where I would be. But, really, I contemplated running to another man. I am deep into this fantasy about sleeping with someone other than my husband." Kenzie's eyes widened. Unlike Gi, this was the first time she had heard any of this. And Kenzie was beyond shocked.

"Oh my God..." Kenzie replied, because she didn't have any other first reaction to knowing the holier-than-thou Lizzy was contemplating having an affair. "You cannot be serious! When did this happen?"

"It's been over the course of the past few months...he's my landscaper." Lizzy creased her brow, and braced for her reaction.

Kenzie giggled at first, but then she stopped herself. "Sorry, that just sounds so forbidden and, well, incredibly sexy."

"Yes!" Lizzy admitted. "My husband is twenty years older than I am. Our sex life has never been all that hot. I am so ashamed to say this, but I want to know what it's like, really like, to be with a man whose body won't quit. I've always hated sex, but these feelings lately…"

"Are making you come alive," Kenzie finished her sentence, and Lizzy exclaimed another *yes!* "Peter and I had amazing sex."

"I know, you've told me," Lizzy used to feel jealous of that, and once would have rolled her eyes. Now, that was no longer appropriate because Peter was gone. "I never have enjoyed it. I mean, I don't want to talk terrible about Max but he's not very attentive."

"I get you," Kenzie said, feeling sorry for Lizzy. "But an affair?"

"I haven't. I've just thought about it. A lot." Lizzy looked away from Kenzie, feeling ashamed, but she realized she had to talk about this. Maybe speaking of it would prevent her from making a mistake. If that's what this was.

"I think you should seek counseling. Maybe start alone, and eventually have Max join you. It takes two, you know, to save a marriage – but only one to sink it," Kenzie stated.

"So you do think my marriage is sinking?" Lizzie asked.

"I'm not sure if I'm qualified to answer that," Kenzie told her. "But, you and Max are."

"Max? He would be floored. He sees us as having it all. A ten-year marriage, a son who we've raised together, money, a great house, expensive vehicles. There is no way that Max would perceive anything about us as needing to be reevaluated or tweaked." Lizzie believed she knew her husband well. And she was spot on.

"I could see that about him, for sure," Kenzie agreed. "But you are in that marriage too. You are not happy, or fulfilled. Having amazing sex with a stranger isn't going to fix this. You have to find another way, a safer, smarter way."

"Hank isn't a stranger," Lizzy said, ignoring Kenzie's implication that she was on the brink of making a thoughtless, rash decision.

"Okay," Kenzie said, giving Lizzy the benefit of the doubt on that one. "Have you talked to Gi about this?"

"Not until we were waiting at the airport for you," Lizzie admitted.

"And what were her thoughts?" Kenzie asked, hoping Gi reacted sensibly.

"First, I think she was really scared for me, like you are," Lizzy answered. "She also wants me to live my life with no regrets. She implied how I will regret cheating, but having mind-blowing sex could be worth it." That was the Gi they both knew. And now Kenzie was concerned that Lizzy would take that dangerous leap because Gi encouraged her.

"Alright, I have one thing to say about your assumption that Hank will satisfy you in ways you've only dreamed about..." Kenzie began. "He could be a disappointment. His dick may be tiny. His stamina may be lost before you're satisfied. You don't know if he will come through for you, pun intended."

"I know how I feel when I am with him, or just thinking about him. The emotion is so intense that I just want to take the risk to feel more." Lizzy sighed.

"Then why are you here? Why didn't you run to this man tonight? Go. Get naked with him and get it over with." As Kenzie spoke, she never took her eyes off of Lizzy. "Don't answer that. I know why, and so do you. It's because you are Lizzy Thomas Zurliene, a woman of integrity. There is no one more genuine. It's not in you to deceive and hurt others."

Lizzie fought back her tears. "Then how do I live with this? How do I keep myself committed to my marriage when I feel like I'm in a rut? After all these years, I've realized I settled for Max to be the one for me."

"You have to talk to Max," Kenzie advised her.

"He's closed-minded and old school," Lizzy supported her reason not to be honest with him.

"He's also your husband," Kenzie reminded her.

A part of Lizzie believed she was right. "Thank you," Lizzie said, giving in, and reaching for Kenzie's hand.

"Actually, thank you. You were successful at getting my mind off of my sorrow tonight," Kenzie told her. "I want to help you through this."

Lizzy wanted to say she wasn't for certain if anyone could help, but instead she remained quiet. She hadn't realized it for a long time, but her faith in Max, in their love, and in their marriage was lost.

Chapter 9

Lizzy contemplated taking Kenzie's advice and having a heart to heart talk with her husband. But this was Max, and Lizzy knew it would be a one-sided conversation that only her heart would be in. She and Max had never connected on a deeper level. Not about anything. Not at all like she and Hank already had. He was attentive with her every word. And right now he was outside of Lizzy's home, hard at work on the landscape.

She toyed with the idea of bringing him a cold drink, but he was a grown man accustomed to working outside in the heat and he always brought his own water cooler. Finally, she went into the kitchen and prepared chicken salad sandwiches and placed those on two plates with pickle spears and potato chips.

Hank immediately looked when Lizzy walked out of her front door. He had just taken several steps out into the yard to observe his own work. It had to look flawless. That's how he completed every job.

"Hi there," he called out to her, and began walking toward the front porch she was stepping off. He wondered if he would see her today. He assumed she was home, given how her vehicle was parked in the open garage.

"Hi," Lizzy responded. "Looking good," she added, referring the landscape but could have easily directed that compliment to him. *Faded grass stained jeans hugged his rear, and his quads. A sleeveless royal blue t-shirt accented the definition in his arms. Sunkissed, sweaty skin. Disheveled blond hair. Stubble on his face.* She obviously was staring too much.

"Thank you. Only the best for you." He smiled. She smiled back.

"Are you hungry? I made lunch." She wanted to say *for us*, but refrained believing that would appear forward. Or worse, desperate.

"Oh, I don't want to impose. Besides I'm way too crummy right now to step inside your home."

"How about chicken salad on my shaded patio?" she suggested.

"Now that sounds like an offer a man shouldn't refuse," he smiled.

"Then don't," Lizzy told him.

✻

This was the first time they had eaten together. They sat close a few times to plan the landscape redo. Max had not been present for those meetings. He had told Lizzy to take the reins because that was her thing. He trusted her judgment. He also trusted her.

But, right now, Max Zurliene felt taken aback as he stood in his kitchen, staring out of the French doors which led outside onto his patio. He came home for lunch with a surprise for his wife. He had just left a local car dealership, driving a brand new black Escalade. Lizzy owned last year's model, but this one was newer with additional expensive features.

Max loosened his cherry red tie around his neck. He hadn't met the landscaper, Hank Stewart. He did know Lizzy went to the same high school as him. Old friends catching up over lunch seemed innocent. That didn't bother Max. What concerned him right now was the way his wife was acting. Or reacting to him. *How she smiled. The conscientious way she held her napkin over her mouth when she spoke while she chewed. She looked different, too. Her long, dark hair was in an updo. She was wearing a sundress. She rarely wore dresses.* She looked so young to Max right now. And smitten.

"It's only going to be another day at the most for me to complete the front yard, and after next week, if the weather cooperates, I should be able to get this done," Hank said, stretching his arm out and pointing in reference to the backyard.

Lizzy wanted to say *take your time*, and tell him there was no rush, because she had gotten used to seeing him every day. "I'm excited about the work you're doing here," she said, instead.

"Well I'm happy you approve," he smiled, as she sat back in his chair and drank the last of the iced tea in his glass.

"Can I get you more to drink?" Lizzy asked him, knowing it would take just a minute to run into the kitchen and get the pitcher out of the refrigerator.

"No thank you," Hank replied. "But, I do appreciate this great lunch. Much better than the turkey wrap I have packed in the cooler."

Lizzy laughed, "Yours sounds healthier though!"

"Healthy can be boring sometimes," Hank stated, but Lizzy knew he took exceptional care of his body. For a moment, she was going to allow herself to feel self-conscious about her fuller figure. But then, she decided against allowing that thought to take over and ruin the moment.

Hank stood up, and started to gather his plate and napkin. "I should be a gentleman and clean up, but I don't want to step foot in your house like this," he frowned, referring to being unclean again.

"Nonsense, I will clean up," Lizzy said, standing up as well. Hank was at least three inches taller than her.

"Thank you again, Elizabeth," Hank said to her, and this time he stared long. He wanted to touch her, tell her she was beautiful. But instead, he walked off the patio and into the grass where he would find his way to the front yard, and back to work.

Lizzy watched him walk away before she stacked their plates and managed to grip both glasses by the rims with her fingers. As she turned around to face the French doors, one of them opened from the inside.

"Let me get the door for you, dear." Lizzy looked up and saw her husband. She felt her heart rate double in just a few seconds, but on the exterior she managed to keep her cool.

"Max, hello. What brings you home in the middle of the day?" Lizzy was instantly worried about how long he had been home, and staring out the kitchen windows.

"Lunch, but I see you've already eaten," he stated. "A burly young landscaper beat me to lunch with my beautiful wife today."

Lizzy smiled, but her teeth were clenched. She had to find her way out of this one. "Oh honey, you know Hank and I are high school friends." Lizzy had hardly known him in high school. He was two years older than her, and he had graduated the year before she became pregnant.

"I do remember you saying that," Max told her. "It was kind of you to make him lunch."

"He's doing great work in our yard," Lizzy attempted to change the subject, to deter her husband from going anywhere inappropriate with this. She felt caught. And guilty enough as it was.

"I agree," Max said, stepping back to watch Lizzy enter the kitchen with the lunch dishes. He walked up behind her when she leaned over the kitchen sink to place the dishes in it. He put his hand on her bottom, and with his other hand he gently moved her hair away from her neck as he placed his lips on her and nuzzled her warm skin.

It was a romantic gesture that Lizzy did not respond to. First, her husband never did anything like that. Sex was just him wanting to touch her quickly and then thrust himself inside of her until he was pleasured. And, just the mere idea of getting it on inside of the house while Hank was right outside was completely out of the question for her.

Lizzy wiggled away from him, and he tried to take in stride how his wife had never looked at him the way he wanted her to. She was sweet, and kind, and loving, toward him always. She just never had a fire for him. Never had she seduced him because she wanted him and desired to be with him. After ten years together, Max had accepted it. *He loved her more, and in a way different way than she loved him.* But after today, when he saw how radiant his wife looked with another man, he wanted her to look at him that way. When he was thirty-eight years old, Lizzy was only eighteen. Max's family and friends told him he was out of his mind to pursue her. He proved them wrong. He won Lizzy over when he offered her a secure life, a father for her son, and anything else she wished for.

"Are you going to eat while you're here for lunch?" Lizzy asked her husband in their kitchen.

"I really want to take you upstairs," he admitted, as he undid the zipper on his dress pants and she saw his hard on through his white briefs. A little blue pill called Viagra often helped him achieve that. Right now, however, he managed on his own. He was driven by knowing he was reaching fifty years old and his wife may be falling for another man twenty years younger than him.

Lizzy giggled. It was more of a nervous giggle, but she tried to hide how she really felt.

"We can't, Max!" she exclaimed, trying to smile at him so he would not see through her. "It wouldn't feel right, knowing we have company right outside, if you know what I mean?"

"I do understand what you mean," he told her. "It wouldn't feel appropriate because the man outside is the one who would be on your mind when I touched you. Isn't that right?" Max asked her, as Lizzy's eyes widened. He zipped up his pants, leaving the bulge of his manhood scrunched behind the material.

"What are you talking about?" Lizzy asked him point-blank, striving to come across as clearly appalled.

"I saw you with him. I watched the two of you for a long time out there. You looked different. You like him, don't you?" Max momentarily held his breath while he waited for his wife to give him an answer.

"Like him? Max we are not in junior high. I had a bite to eat with an old friend who happens to be doing some amazing landscape work in our yard. Are you accusing me of something more? You think I'm having an affair just because I wouldn't lift up my dress for you right now?"

"I'm not saying you have done anything," Max answered, "but are you denying that you want to?"

This was Lizzy's chance. She needed to take it. Never before would she have thought to have Max's undivided attention this way. That's what Kenzie told her to do. *Be honest. Communicate your wants and needs. Work on the pitfalls in your marriage.*

"What I want is some space," she told him, completely ignoring the little voice in her head. *The one that wanted her to fight to save her marriage, and the only life she knew.*

"From me?" Max asked her.

"From us," she replied, holding her own, while her insides quivered something fierce.

"I bought you a new Escalade today," he said, suddenly ignoring the serious conversation they were having.

"What?" she frowned. *Had he even heard her?*

"It's on the driveway. I'll drive your old one back to the dealership when I leave. It's all yours, complete with the bells and whistles you are used to having in this life that you share with me." Max was desperately trying to drive his point home.

"I don't need a new vehicle," she told him.

"Do you need this big house? Do you need our bank account?" Max raised his voice to her. "And what about our son?" Max played the card he always knew he would have the power to use, if it came down to it. But, honestly, he never thought their lives would ever have to be divvied up to his and hers.

"You are making no sense whatsoever!" Lizzy yelled at him. "Griffin is our son, and he always will be." Lizzy wondered if Max needed to be reminded how he was the only father her son had ever known. Max had given her and Griffin everything.

"I know that. I gave that boy my name, and raised him as my own. He's mine in every sense of the word," Max stated, as Lizzy nodded her head in agreement. "So, if you were to need *space* or, as we attorneys like to call it, a separation – the boy stays with me."

Lizzy's eyes widened. She wanted to say to him that he could not do that. *Biologically, Griffin was hers.* This scared her. She hadn't felt this terrified since the moment she was pregnant and alone at sixteen.

"Your silence tells me that you understand," Max stated callously. There was a definite heartlessness to this man which Lizzy had never witnessed before.

"All I implied was that maybe you and I need to reevaluate us, our marriage," Lizzy boldly told him.

"I bought you a new vehicle. I wanted to make love to you in the middle of the day. I'm openly communicating with you. Those are all good qualities in a husband. Don't you think so, Liz?" Max asked her, as she felt a chill shoot through her entire body. *He was in lawyer mode.*

Lizzy didn't respond. She only nodded her head as if she was in agreement. She felt so strange at this moment. This man who she was married to, lived with, and cared about for the past decade now seemed incredibly unfamiliar to her. She suddenly feared him. Or, she at least feared what he –the successful attorney– could take away from her. *Her son.*

Chapter 10

Four hours earlier, Gi had pounded on the front door of Kenzie's condo. After two rings of her doorbell, she resorted to using her fist. Nonstop. Until Kenzie answered. Gi knew she was home, because her car was parked out front.

From the other side, Kenzie turned the deadbolt lock and opened the door. Gi looked at her before she said anything. She was still wearing the same dress she had on twenty-four hours ago when her plane landed at the airport. Her hair remained in a knotty updo. If she had been wearing any makeup, she had long cried it all off. Her eyes were red and her face was puffy.

"What are doing banging on my door so early?" Kenzie spoke first.

"It's not early. Children are already at school. People are at work," Gi told her, pushing past her through the doorway.

"Then you should be at work." Kenzie's attitude was snarky, and Gi believed she had every right to hate the world and everyone in it. But that was a hole she would only sink deeper into if Gi didn't pull her out now. There were at least three empty wine bottles on the coffee table in front of the sofa that Gi was looking at when Kenzie walked past her and plopped down on the sofa, where it was obvious she had been all night long.

"I should have stayed here last night," Gi said, feeling both certain and regretful.

"It's fine. I'm fine. Lizzy came by for awhile," Kenzie told her.

"Now I really feel bad about not being here," Gi said, rolling her eyes at herself.

"No need to. I think Lizzy needed me more than I did her, if you can believe that," Kenzie stated.

"Oh boy...so you know about Hunky Hank?" Gi asked, still standing on the opposite end of the coffee table.

"Do I ever," she answered. "It's unbelievable to see her acting this way – about a man. I mean, I really think she's going to risk everything."

"Me too," Gi agreed. "Unless we stop her."

"When she's ripping off this new guy's clothes, the last thing she is going to be thinking about is us, my friend," Kenzie said, and she actually laughed after spoke.

Gi giggled at the thought, "You're right."

"Maybe we can gang up on her and talk some more sense into her, together this time, after work today?" Kenzie suggested.

"Are you going to work?" Gi asked.

"You, not me," Kenzie corrected her.

"Why not you? Don't you have clients relying on you?" Gi put her on the spot. Kenzie was a psychiatrist at Lake Regional Health in Osage Beach. In just a few short years, her career had brought her success and prestige. Kenzie was proud of who she had worked very hard to become – and Gi made an attempt to reach her that way.

"My husband just died. Not to mention, I'm supposed to still be on my honeymoon," Kenzie reminded her.

"True," Gi said, "but you may need to focus on work soon," Gi picked up one of the wine bottles on the table. "You're drinking too much and you haven't taken a shower or changed out of that dress in too long. Start taking better care of yourself, or things will get worse."

"Jesus, Gi! Let me grieve. Let me drink. Who cares if I don't want to take care of myself for awhile? It's warranted, don't you think?" Kenzie was angry, and Gi wanted to see that reaction from her. She wanted her to feel. It was time to get mad, and just react, before she lost too much of herself.

"There you go!" Gi raised her voice back at Kenzie. "Let it out."

"You want me to feel?" Kenzie actually laughed. "That's rich, considering I'm the one who gets paid to make other people feel, and talk it out."

"Go on..." Gi told her, as she moved another bottle of wine aside on the table and sat down on the edge. She was now directly in front of Kenzie, on her level and face-to-face. No matter how hard Gi was trying to give her tough love right now, Kenzie could see the sensitivity and the affection in her eyes. And that was what made Kenzie cave.

"Without him, I do not know what to do with myself, or who I even am anymore," she began. "What Peter and I were together, the life we hardly had a chance to create was better than anything I've done alone." Kenzie began to cry, and Gi moved toward her so swiftly, it at first surprised her. But when they embraced, Kenzie held on for dear life.

"That was such a beautiful way to describe your love," Gi nearly whispered those words, because she too felt like crying for her best friend's great loss. "I am so sorry for your pain, but I'm going to make it my purpose to pull your ass through this."

Kenzie smiled through her tears. "Well we all know how crazy you get when you have a purpose."

"That's right," Gi winked at her. "I don't stop until I attain what I'm after."

"If you manage that feat, I'll love you the most," Kenzie said, referring to their trinity. They all had taken their turn over the years saying they loved one more than the other at specific times.

"I am not going to do anything," Gi stated. "You are. It's up to you. You're not alone, and you never will be. You are stuck with me and Lizzy. But, you have to take charge of your life. Stand up…"

Kenzie did as Gi asked. She stood directly in front of her in her bare feet and that ankle-length light gray dress.

"Raise up your arms," Gi instructed her, and Kenzie did so. Gi bent down and grabbed the end of her dress and pulled it all the way up and over her body and finally over her head. She wadded up the dress and threw it onto the sofa. Kenzie stood there in her racerback laced black bra and matching panties.

"Now what? Your turn?" Kenzie winked at her, and they both giggled.

Gi slapped Kenzie's rear end. "Go take a shower."

"I'm going," Kenzie halfheartedly inched her way in the direction of the bathroom.

"I'll be here when you get done. Count on that." Gi called after her, as she started to clean up the empty bottles on the coffee table. Gi needed to make herself useful and not just sit there, dwelling on how that condo just didn't feel the same to her either. Not without Peter racing from room to room with that goofy smile on his face.

✱

It was pouring down rain, the kind of rainfall which felt uncomfortable if you were unshielded from it. And Gi and Kenzie currently were on the receiving end of the slanted downpour that fell on them as they ran up the driveway and onto the front porch of Lizzy's house. She was the only one home, as Griffin was in school and Max was working. And her landscaper obviously wasn't working in the soggy yard today.

When Lizzy rushed to open her door to whomever was standing out in the rain, she was pleasantly surprised to see Gi and Kenzie staring back at her.

"Come in you two! Holy Moly it's a mess out there."

Lizzy grabbed towels from her linen closet upstairs so they could dry off and be comfortable. The three of them sat perched on the high stools around Lizzy's kitchen island, where stainless steel pots and pans hung above them – just like on all of the classy cooking shows on television. When Gi looked up at those pots and pans, she wondered what she always did, *were those ever used, or just hanging up there for show?*

"Can I get you two something to eat or drink? Would either of you prefer something strong?" Lizzy asked, feeling like she needed alcohol ever since yesterday's dealings with her husband.

"Ugh, no, not me," Kenzie spoke up. "I seriously need to detox for a day or two."

"Coffee?" Lizzy offered, and Kenzie nodded.

"I'll have what you're having," Gi chimed in.

"Vodka," Lizzy told her, and both Gi and Kenzie instantly knew something was wrong. Lizzy remained the straight arrow, and among the three of them she was always the one to just give in and go along with their shenanigans, including drinking.

"You better start talking," Gi told Lizzy, as she sat down after preparing two Bloody Marys and one black coffee poured from the fresh pot she already had brewed this morning.

"No. This morning should be about Kenz," Lizzy said, as she held Kenzie's eyes for a meaningful moment. It was to be expected, but Lizzy thought Kenzie looked awful. *Haggard. Drained. And terribly sad.*

"Oh please, what did I tell you last night? The two of you need to keep my mind busy on the happenings in your lives so I feel like I'm still living. A part of me did die with Peter. I know that. But I'm going to try really hard to keep myself afloat. I will keep his memory alive, if it kills me." They all three laughed. It wasn't funny. It was true though. Grief could make those left behind feel as if they too were dying.

"Well I'm afraid the happenings in my life are going to seem pretty damn unbelievable right now," Lizzy admitted. "I'm in a huge mess." She looked down at her Bloody Mary. She had yet to take a sip of it.

"You didn't, did you?" Gi asked, and they all knew what she was referring to.

"Max caught me," she began, while Kenzie gasped and Gi blurted out *Holy shit!* "Not that," Lizzy was quick to correct their initial assumption. "I prepared lunch here while Hank was doing the landscaping. I invited him to eat with me on the patio. Max came home early to surprise me with yet another new vehicle."

"What did he see?" Kenzie asked.

"And what did he say?" Gi chimed in.

"I didn't know he was there, standing in front of the windows or the French doors watching us. When I came inside after Hank went back to work, Max confronted me. He said it was not a big deal to find me having lunch with a high school friend, but what caught his attention and bothered him, he said, was the way I looked at Hank, and how I reacted to him. Jesus, I know I'm infatuated, but did I have to be that obvious?"

"Well you didn't know your husband was watching," Gi defended her.

"No, I didn't," Lizzy agreed.

"So were you able to make nothing of it and settle Max down?" Kenzie asked.

"I thought so, at first," Lizzy stated, "but then he came onto me, seriously he had a hard on right here in the kitchen. That hasn't happened in years!" The three of them laughed out loud before Lizzy continued. "We shouldn't laugh because there really is no humor in this at all. He was angry that I rejected him for afternoon sex. I guess that was his way of testing me, you know to see if I really am attracted to Hank. I ended up telling him that I need some space. And it was almost as if he became someone else. He threatened me. He reminded me of the no holds barred attorney that he is, and he said if I were to leave him, Griffin stays with him."

"No. No way. Griffin is not biologically his!" Gi spat those words. This hit home for her. Her little girl was the reason she had stayed in a loveless marriage. Ric was indeed Suzie's biological father and she adored him as much as he did her. In Lizzy's case, Gi believed Griffin needed his mother more. Max was a provider, but he wasn't Griffin's blood and he couldn't take him away from Lizzy. And besides, Gi had done her share of sleeping around and so-called living before she got married. Lizzy never had. So, in Gi's mind, that fact made Lizzy's situation altogether different than her own. Gi no longer wanted or needed a man. She only cared about keeping her little girl happy, and giving her a stable life she never had growing up.

"I was afraid to pursue this, but it was almost as if Max already had this in the bag. As if there are papers lined up and ready to file. I suddenly didn't trust him." Lizzy swallowed hard. Her mouth was dry and her stomach was upset.

"Oh my God," Kenzie spoke softly. "So you're saying you're stuck?"

"I don't know," Lizzy admitted.

"You cannot live in fear of him. You have rights. Yes, he is an attorney and a damn good one, but there are other attorneys who specialize in divorce who can help you," Gi was adamant.

"But I never said I wanted a divorce," Lizzy stated. "I just need to work through these feelings."

"You're contemplating having an affair, Liz," Kenzie told her outright. "That's hardly working through your feelings."

"Yeah I guess that didn't come out right," Lizzy said, knowing she should feel ashamed, but she didn't.

"So, have you told Hank?" Gi asked.

"Absolutely not, but don't think I didn't contemplate going to him and just laying all of the cards of the table," Lizzy admitted.

"Or laying him down," Gi interjected and laughed before the other two did.

"That, too," Lizzy said, feeling her cheeks flush a bit. "Tell me what I should do. At this point I see myself stuck in my marriage, daydreaming about what could have been with someone else, but never really doing anything about it."

"Let me go first," Gi said, looking at Kenzie, and she nodded. She was the professional and already had her answer in her head anyway. She could wait her turn. "I am stuck because I choose to be. I do not love Ric anymore, but Suzie does. I know I'll leave him one day, when my little girl doesn't need her mommy and daddy under the same roof. I will sacrifice my happiness for hers for as long as I need to."

"That's just wrong," Kenzie interrupted her.

"We are not talking about me," Gi bluntly reminded her.

"I just have one thing to say about that before you can continue," Kenzie spoke again. "Look at what happened to me. It hurts so much right now, but I realize I had the greatest love I'll probably ever know. I was given the chance to experience that, and it's something I'll always cherish. You both are depriving yourselves of that. Okay, that's it. I'm done. Go on."

Gi and Lizzy both looked at each other and then back at Kenzie. She was not only a gifted professional in her field, who always had the right answers and a definite way to guide people in the healthy, fruitful direction. She also was the one person who knew Gi and Lizzy the best. And she loved them anyway. Just as they did her. Kenzie was hardly perfect.

"As I was saying," Gi continued. "I am trapped by choice. You are going to be stuck because your husband has turned into even more of a control freak than he was before. It's one thing to provide for you – and then some," Gi said looking around Lizzy's massive, extravagant kitchen, "but it's another to force you to stay with him because he thinks he has convinced you that you will lose your son. *Your* son!"

"Do not let him take Griffin," Kenzie added her opinion. "Fight him."

"Girls…" Lizzy spoke softly. "I have nothing to show for. I've never worked a day in my life. I have no higher education degree. Max knows he holds all of the power over me."

"What about to be a mother to your son?" Kenzie asked. "Max cannot be that for Griffin. And, you're right, you have not done anything *for you* since the day you gave birth to your baby when you were still a baby yourself. But, I strongly disagree with you. You have everything *to show for* when it comes to being a wonderful, caring, nurturing mother. You better believe that counts for something."

Lizzy reached for Kenzie's hand from across the granite countertop of the island. "Thank you. You both have once again pumped me full of courage. I can do this. I need to make some changes in my life."

Chapter 11

Lizzy fell back into her life without altering anything. A week went by and the landscaping around her entire yard was complete – and it looked amazing. But Lizzy never told Hank as much. In fact, she had not seen him. She avoided him by leaving the house every morning before he showed up, and coming home late in the afternoon when he was finished working for the day and already left. He had texted her a few times, mostly about business. Only once did he mention how he hoped to catch her at home before his job for her was finished.

Both Kenzie and Gi knew what Lizzy was doing. She was afraid, so she had fallen back into the place where she felt familiar and safe. Being Max's wife. Going above and beyond to be a good mother to Griffin. She believed removing Hank from her life would allow her to return to who she used to be. But she could not have been more wrong.

✱

After a quick trip to the grocery store for dinner ingredients ninety minutes before Griffin was expected home from a friend's house and Max was due home from work, Lizzy was pushing her cart through the parking lot when she spotted his truck. She stared for a long moment, trying to see if he was inside of it. *Had he just now driven into the lot and parked in that spot? Did she luck out and already miss him going inside of the store as she was checking out her groceries and leaving?*

Before another thought entered her mind, Lizzy saw the driver's side door open, and those long, muscular legs in denim were visible first. She thought about picking up her pace, moving right on by, just three spaces down where she was parked. But then Hank saw her.

"Hello Elizabeth," he said first, closing his truck door behind him. Hank smiled, but there was something distant about him. Lizzy immediately assumed her avoidance last week had upset him.

"Hi," she replied, walking behind her cart to meet him at the tailgate of his truck.

"I missed you last week," he said, immediately expressing how he felt. And that was why she adored this man. He said what was on his mind…or in his heart. Lizzy sure did wonder what really was going on in that big heart of his.

"I know, me too," she replied. "I'm sorry. Last week was just so hectic. The yard looks wonderful, thank you. Oh, and your check, I mailed it. You should be getting it in a day or so."

"Got it already," he replied. "Thank you."

"No, thank you. Seriously, I'm really happy with it."

Lizzy glanced at him and then quickly looked down at the ground at her feet.

"And your husband?" Hank brought up Max. He never brought up Max.

"What about him?" Lizzy asked.

"Does he like the landscape in his yard?" Hank clarified.

"Oh, right! Yes, yes he does. Thank you." This conversation was so awkward and completely unlike all of the other exchanges between them. And Lizzy felt overwhelmed with guilt. She was the reason there was a wall between them right now. She had been downright rude to him. But she had to drop him, cold turkey, if she was going to get over how she felt.

"What's for dinner tonight?" he asked her, looking into the two grocery bags, packed and sitting side by side in the grocery cart.

"Um, spaghetti, a tossed salad, and a well, wine," she laughed. "What about you?" They were meeting halfway again. The aura was slowly reaching comfortable between them.

"Just wine," he laughed. "I'm here for a bottle to go with the pizza I'll order later."

"Sounds wonderful," Lizzy said, reminding herself that he was a bachelor, but it did surprise her that he wasn't eating healthy. She assumed he must work out at the gym like crazy to maintain a body without an ounce of visible fat. She imagined him running on a treadmill, or doing some sort of cardio that made him sweat profusely. She was at it again. *That man and her daydreams.*

"Have a glass with me," he suggested, and Lizzy immediately felt surprised. This was not at all in her plan. She had put distance between them, and now Hank was making it very hard for her to keep it up.

Use the excuse that you have to make dinner for your family. "Now?" she heard herself ask him after she deliberately ignored her conscious. And she had a very strong feeling that if she agreed to have a drink with this man, her conscious was going to end up being a guilty one.

"Sure, why not?" Hank asked her. "It's early yet, spaghetti takes what? Thirty minutes, tops, to prepare? Have your wine before your meal, with me." Lizzy was searching her mind for a reason not to. Of course she knew why she should refuse this man, but she couldn't tell him the truth. *Could she?*

"I'll be late, my family will be waiting on me," she said, sensibly, and then she could have kicked herself. *Who was going to be waiting if she was not on time? Griffin was always late, after choosing to spend more time with his friends. She even wondered lately if he had a girlfriend he was meeting with. There had been an awful lot of time spent at friend's houses lately. And she did smell cologne on him a few times at the breakfast table. And then she thought of Max. He could have a case that needed his attention after five-thirty.*

Lizzy decided to take that risk. "I already have the wine. I'll follow you."

Hank nodded his head. It almost seemed as if he was surprised she had said yes. "Okay then. Let's go."

Lizzy's heart was about to pound out of her chest as she placed her grocery bags in the backseat of her SUV and then slipped into the driver's seat. She could hear Gi saying – *just do it, you only live once for chrissakes!* And she also heard the ringing of Kenzie's warning in her ears. *You are Lizzy Thomas Zurliene, a woman of integrity. There is no one more genuine. It's not in you to deceive and hurt others.* And finally, she remembered Max turning on her in their kitchen. He was controlling and he held so much power over her head. Since that day, Lizzy had tried very hard to go back to who she was before. And it was as if Max was banking on that. Too many times in the last week he had popped those little blue pills before they went to bed at night. Lizzy felt sickened and entirely used. She hated him for how he had her trapped now. His touch had repulsed her. That was her final thought, her reasoning behind following Hank home, as she drove behind him into the parking lot of his apartment complex.

*

Hank's apartment was small, but very neat and tidy. There was wood flooring in both the kitchen and living areas. His taste in furniture –an all black leather recliner and sofa with wrought iron glass-topped tables– and stainless steel kitchen appliances immediately caught Lizzy's attention. She also liked how in the corner of his living room he had puzzles, toys and a miniature kitchen set, all for when his two-and-a-half-year-old little girl stayed with him two days a week and every other weekend. Hank didn't talk about Annie unless Lizzy brought her up. And every time she asked, he beamed with pride when he spoke of her.

Lizzy sat down at the kitchen table after Hank took the bottle of wine from her and walked over to the kitchen counter to uncork it and retrieve two glasses. "When will you see Annie again?" she asked him, wishing she had felt uncomfortable being in his home. It would have been easier to justify that this was wrong. But, right now, it felt far from something she shouldn't be doing.

"She was just with me last night, and my weekend with her is coming up again," Hank smiled. "I enjoy when you ask about her."

"Oh I'm sure everyone who knows her asks about her. She's adorable in the pictures you've shown me," Lizzy stated, and he smiled.

"It's hard to have a child – and date," Hank added.

"I'm sure it is," Lizzy said, but she couldn't entirely relate because when she was a single mother, she never dated. She met Max by chance, he knew her situation, and he pursued her. Max had made her life incredibly easy. But she never truly loved him. "So, do you date?"

"A little, but it seems like I know immediately if it's going to work or not. I want to feel like I could talk to her all night long. The connection has to be natural and true and deep. Like it is with us."

Hank surprised Lizzy with what he just came right out and said. "I guess it's easier when two people are friends," Lizzy said, taking a long swallow of her wine. And it immediately went to her head. She wanted to feel a little drunk right now.

"I agree," Max said, also taking a generous swallow from his glass. And then he reached across the table and touched her hand. "Are you happy in your marriage?"

"That's not a fair question," Lizzy told him, and looked away.

"It's an honest one though. You're here. And I want to know why. We're friends, yes. But could there be more? That's why I asked you here. We need to talk about this."

"I'm married," she reminded him. Or maybe she was giving herself a stern reminder of her wedding vows.

"Happily?" Hank asked her once again.

"Comfortably," she answered, as she began to say more, "to a man who saved me in so many ways. Without him, I never would have been able to give my son the life we have, the father he has."

"That's important," Hank stated. "Our children come first."

Lizzy nodded her head. "But when we allow ourselves to fall by the wayside, who will care? I mean, really, who will be there for us?"

"I think you already know the answer to that," Hank told her. "That's when we stand up for ourselves, and we do something that makes us happy. Is that selfish? Or right or wrong? Who knows for sure what it is really. We just go after it if it's what we want."

"What if it feels crazy, or it ends up being a risk I should not take?" Lizzy asked him.

"I would never intentionally hurt you, Elizabeth," he spoke without taking his eyes off of her, and he was still touching her hand.

"I don't know if I can say the same. I'm drawn to you for more than one reason, but I'm still a married woman and a mother to a boy that I don't want to disappoint." Lizzy continued to allow Hank to hold her hand in his. That simple gesture was electrifying.

"Then we take this one moment at a time. No expectations," Hank told her, leaning toward her. Their faces were very close, and their hands were still intertwined on the table.

She wanted to meet his lips with hers. She needed to feel the intensity of a passion she had never before known, because deep in her soul right now she knew this was it. All she had to do was give in. Even if it was only for a little while, Lizzy wanted to chase this feeling.

But she was terrified, that if she did, she would never be able to let go when she had to. There would be more pain in leaving this man after she fell in love with him. The attraction, the lust, and the wonderment of what could be with him was why she befriended him, daydreamed about him, and finally followed him there tonight. And now she was going to leave the same way. Still not knowing what they could be.

Chapter 12

Kenzie sat behind her desk in her spacious office in Osage Beach at Lake Regional Health, a hospital where she began her career directly out of college four years ago.

It had been two weeks since Peter's death, and seventeen days since their wedding day. She was supposed to be a newlywed, but instead she was a widow.

There were patients on her schedule today, and while she dreaded pushing herself through this day, she also knew how badly she needed to be back at work and productive again. It was like she was starting all over with her life. Back to a time when she had a career, but no one to go home to.

In front of her on the cherry wood desktop were pictures. Thank goodness they had captured so much of their time together. Bike rides, Major League Baseball games in St. Louis, walks in the park, late-night dinners. Kenzie took a hold of one of the frames. They had just completed a twenty-mile bike ride and parked their bikes and plopped down in the grass. Their faces were close for that selfie. And Peter, who Kenzie laughed softly at right now, was still wearing his bike helmet. He looked so silly. A goofy grin. His wavy brown hair peeking out like wings from the helmet's gaps.

"I want to be that happy again," Kenzie heard herself say aloud, and she was speaking to him. "But, you know as well as I do...I am going to be in love with you for the rest of my life."

The intercom on her desk phone interrupted her. It was her administrative assistant, Alisa and her first patient had arrived. Kenzie told her to send him in.

There was no file for this new patient. Alisa had said he called twice while she was on leave. His name was Tony Carter. His reason for scheduling an appointment was he was *ready to accept responsibility for his actions in order to change his life for the better.* That was quite a bit of detail to give out before a session. He also had been insistent on seeing Dr. MacKenzie Wade. Kenzie was still going by her maiden name. She was Kenzie Sterling on paper now, but she just didn't think she could handle hearing herself called Dr. Sterling all day long. So, Dr. Wade she would remain.

"Dr. Wade," Alisa said, opening her office door, "Tony Carter is here to see you."

Kenzie was already standing behind her desk, wearing her white physician's coat, which ended in unison with her short skirt today. When he stepped into her office, Alisa closed the door and left them alone. Kenzie, at first, wore her professsional smile. This was the part where she normally would extend her hand and invite her patient to sit down. But she didn't. Not yet.

Sometimes through the years people will forget faces and especially names as time passes and life moves on. Not this time. Not this face. And Tony Carter was not his name.

"Trey Toennies?" Kenzie spoke his name in the form of a question, but she already knew the answer. It was him. Tall. Still had an athletic build, but his waistline seemed narrower. That familiar thick chest and a full head of dark hair, which he kept much shorter and gelled now.

"Kenzie," he spoke her name just like he used to. High school suddenly seemed so much longer ago than just a little more than a decade. But it had been that long since this man was her boyfriend. They had only dated for six months. They had gone all the way, but Trey Toennies had not been the one Kenzie gave her virginity to. That girl was Lizzy.

"Why are you here, and lying to me about your name?" Kenzie paused before she said anything more. She was a professional. She couldn't judge him. But the pain he caused her had surfaced. He lied to her all those years ago when he told her she was the only girl he wanted to touch for the rest of his life. That seemed so trivial now. They were just hormonal teenagers. They hadn't really been in love.

This man, who was actually just an overgrown boy when Kenzie knew him, had caused quite a rift between her and Lizzy.

Lizzy, of course, had never been more remorseful in all her life. Her actions had cost her dearly. Sleeping with a boy for the first time had caused her to get pregnant – and lose her best friend. Kenzie vowed to never speak to her again. And eventually, after too many harsh words and a flood of tears, it was Gi who convinced Kenzie how their friendship –their trinity– was a whole lot more meaningful than some jock who only wanted to get laid and had really used them both.

"I apologize for that, but would you have agreed to see me if you had known it was me?" Trey asked her.

"Good point," Kenzie replied.

"Can I sit down?" he asked her, taking small steps toward the desk she was still standing behind.

"You may as well," she answered, as she too sat in her chair she thought again of what Alisa had told her about the man who had called twice, requesting to see her. *He wanted to accept responsibility for his actions in order to change his life for the better.* This wasn't Kenzie's first rodeo. Most of her patients who came to see her needed to face, work through, and eventually accept or make changes with something that occurred in their past. Kenzie picked up her pencil and then dropped it back down on her desktop, as she inhaled a deep breath and thought of Griffin.

Trey crossed one leg over the other, sort of like a gentleman would sit. Not at all like a jock, like the boy she remembered him as being. Maybe he, like the rest of them, had matured. He wore a white button-down shirt untucked into dark-washed denim with brown leather loafers on his bare feet. Casual, but classy. But, this guy wasn't a class act, Kenzie reminded herself. Despite the fact that he was a teenager with a mother who pushed him to purse a college career on a sports scholarship, he had abandoned his baby.

"I should start by telling you why I'm here," Trey began, and Kenzie only stared back at him. This was no longer a professional session. She, at least, was not going to treat it like one. If Trey Toennies wanted a piece of her time this way, he got it. And now he had fifty-seven minutes left in the hour she was charging him for. "I'm almost thirty years old, I'm a high school teacher and basketball coach in Boston. I've never gotten married, and I just got out of really serious relationship. My girlfriend and I were living together, and then she left me because I couldn't commit to her. That isn't the first time this has happened in my life. I've loved and lost before because the idea of making a commitment –marriage and having children– is keeping me from having a life with someone."

Kenzie was surprised to hear Trey admit this. Most men, like him, lived in denial that it was their fault when a woman accused them of having commitment issues. Most of those men lived out their entire lives as bachelors. "So, you are here for my help? You want to change this about yourself?"

"Yes and no," Trey answered her. "I do need your help, but I'm not asking for your wisdom, or guidance. I just need you."

"I don't understand," Kenzie admitted, but again she thought of Griffin – and Lizzy.

"I want to meet my son. I want to get to know him. He's gotta be twelve now, right? I think it's time I own up to what I did, and try to make it right. You and Lizzy were so close, I assume you still are. I actually know you are. You both are pictured in each other's public posts on Facebook."

"Ahhh, so you've done a little investigating," Kenzie spoke without showing any kind of expression on her face. "And you're here to use me as some sort of middle person. If I put in a good word for you with Lizzy, you think she will allow you to meet *her* son?" Kenzie stressed *her*. Griffin was hers. And Max's.

"Something like that, yes," Trey replied.

"You know, you may look a little different – better actually," Kenzie admitted, still keeping her face expressionless, "but you're still a component of the male species with some serious balls. You and I were dating, seriously, I might add. You slept with my best friend, got her pregnant, and without a second thought you abandoned your baby. And, now, here you are twelve years later, asking the girlfriend you screwed around on to help you?"

"I know how to swallow my pride. I also know how to apologize. We were just kids, Kenz." She didn't want him to call her that. Peter used to call her that. And now only Gi and Lizzy do. "It's not too late for me to make this right, is it?"

Kenzie thought about her answer before she said anything at all. *Griffin had a father in his life, who had given him a wonderful, stable environment to grow up in. Kenzie knew for certain Max loved his son, and Griffin loved him. Kenzie also thought about what Lizzy had been going through the last few months. Would Max really take her son away if Lizzy left him? Not if he had two biological parents in his life. Successful attorney or not, no judge would grant custody of a child to the adoptive father.*

"I don't know if you can right this wrong," Kenzie said, honestly, "but I will talk to Lizzy for you."

Chapter 13

Trey left his cell phone number with Kenzie and informed her that he would be staying with his mother in Lake Ozark for the next few days. Kenzie had a deadline. She knew she needed to tell Lizzy that her son's biological father was back in town. And worse, he wanted to meet Griffin.

Kenzie fretted about her decision once she agreed to this, but something spur of the moment inside of her had told her to do it. And it had everything to do with Max's recent treatment towards Lizzy. Whether Lizzy would agree to any of it remained to be seen.

✱

"She is going to kill you," Gi told Kenzie on their way to Lizzy's house after they had both wrapped up a work day. Kenzie was driving and she gripped both of her hands tighter around the steering wheel when Gi's reaction made her more nervous about telling Lizzy.

Lizzy was home alone most early evenings, and Kenzie had called ahead to tell her they were going to stop by.

"Stop saying that," Kenzie told her again. "I think this could be a good thing if everyone just opens up their minds to the idea."

"The idea? You speak of this as if it's just a lighthearted thing. It's not. Kenz, no offense but you do not have a child of your own yet. You have absolutely no idea what it feels like to want and need to protect them. This could get ugly. Griffin could get hurt."

"That's not fair," Kenzie replied. "I'm thinking about Lizzy's child and how her husband threatened to take him away. Just stop stressing me out even more over this. It's ultimately Lizzy's decision anyway. She could easily tell me to tell Trey to fuck off and that would be the end of it."

"True," Gi agreed. "I just think Lizzy has too much on her plate right now as it is. And, Griffin is at such an awkward age. Change like this could really effect him."

"Maybe this is what Lizzy needs to make a change in her life. I just feel like Max has her backed into a corner and she's given up," Kenzie spoke with serious concern in her voice. "And Grif is a big boy. He knows he's loved. And what do we know, maybe he's had thoughts of wanting to meet his biological father? Lizzy has always been open and honest with him about Max adopting him when he was just two."

"I understand. You do make some valid points," Gi told Kenzie. "I'm just damn curious about something..."

"Go on," Kenzie said, as they pulled onto Lizzy's driveway.

"Why are you giving Trey Toennies the time of day after what he did to you?" Gi asked, as Kenzie shut off the engine.

"Two reasons," she began. "We were just kids then, making stupid mistakes without thinking about each other's feelings."

"And your second reason?" Gi asked, after Kenzie paused when she opened her car door to get out.

"I know how to forgive."

✱

The three of them were in their usual spots around the kitchen island in Lizzy's home. It didn't matter where they gathered, it never had, but lately they were there, in that extravagant house, and focused on Lizzy. Just weeks ago, it appeared as if they would be at Kenzie's condo and the tragic events in her life would consume all of them, but that hadn't been the case. Kenzie was forcing herself to focus on others. And now, Gi worried that she may have gone too far.

Lizzy offered them a plate to sample the dinner she had cooking, or wine, but they both declined. She instantly sat down and asked, *what's going on?*

Gi looked at Kenzie and she began talking.

"I had a new patient show up at my office this morning," she told Lizzy. "He used a false name to schedule an appointment. I took one look at him and knew he was Trey Toennies."

First, Lizzy flushed from her neck upward, then the color slowly drained from her face. "What? No. Why is he back? And why did he want to see you?" In all the years, Lizzy wondered if Trey Toennies would ever return to his home town. The first two years of Griffin's life, she used to lie awake and night and imagine him showing up and having changed his mind, wanting to be a part of his son's life. After she met and married Max, she thought less and less about Griffin's birth father.

"He told me that he's living in Boston, where he's a high school teacher and coach," Lizzy stated as Gi kept quiet, already having heard all of this on their drive there. "He's never been married, just girlfriends who have left him because he has a serious fear of commitment. Marriage, and especially having kids, apparently scares the hell out of him."

"Obviously - since he has a son he's never met." As Lizzy said those words, she watched both of her friend's facial expressions change. "No. No!" Lizzy knew what was coming next, and she wasn't going to hear of it.

"He said he wants to meet his son...and maybe get to know him," Kenzie swallowed hard. Now she wished she had that glass of wine.

"I said no!" Lizzy raised her voice, leaped off of her stool, and stood facing out the large corner windows behind the stainless steel sink.

"I told you," Gi uttered quietly to Kenzie, and Lizzy turned around to face them again.

"Why you?" Lizzy asked Kenzie. "Doesn't he know that you hate him?"

"I didn't welcome him into my office with open arms, Liz," Kenzie spoke, gently. "But, I did hear him out. And I did, eventually, agree to tell you this. I'm not at all on his side. It's Trinity against the world, everyone who knows us, or has seen us together for more than five minutes, is aware of that fact." Lizzy continued to listen to Kenzie. "I was ready to tell him to get out, out of my office, out of this town, and to forget the idea of meeting Griffin. But then, I thought of you. I thought of the craziness you're going through with Max. You're staying with him because he threatened to take Max away from you – and you believe he could. Well what if Trey–"

"Oh my God! No! What were you thinking? Shared custody between here and Boston? I've given my life to that boy. Where the hell has Trey been for all that time? No. Since you're so fucking chummy with him again, you can give him that message!"

Lizzy turned her back to them again, and then she leaned over the kitchen sink and cried. Both Kenzie and Gi instantly got on their feet and met her with their arms.

"I'm sorry," Kenzie spoke first in their huddle.

"You should be," Gi scolded her, and Kenzie shoved her out of their embrace. They all three, in turn, giggled – even Lizzy through her tears.

"He's leaving town in a few days. I have his number. I'll tell him." While Kenzie respected Lizzy's adamant wishes, she still had a strong feeling which would not subside. There was a reason Trey showed up, his timing had to mean something.

"You know," Lizzy began speaking, and her tone easily echoed how she had something important to share with them. "Grif looks like me. He always has. But, there are traits he has that are his father's. Look how that boy handles a basketball." The three of them smiled. Lizzy had never admitted that before. "But, he's not his father. I am doing the right thing. Max loves him like his own."

Kenzie nodded her head. She would just agree with Lizzy on this subject from here on. She had already done enough damage. This time, however, Gi offered her opinion.

"Of course Max loves Grif. We all do," Gi began. "Max is great with opening his wallet. Both you and Grif have not wanted for anything, material-wise, since that man waltzed in your lives. But, honesty, has Max ever played a game, gone fishing, or just bonded over anything with Grif? Same with you, Lizzy. He's your husband, but you're not in love with him. You never were. Just think about this. There's a man who made a decision when he was basically just a boy. He sees the error of his ways now. One meeting? You could insist on being present. Grif may need that man in his life more than you realize. Or, I could be way off. Talk to your son."

Lizzy sighed, as Kenzie was staring at Gi with tears in her eyes. *What an amazing gift from God. The three of them in this life together.*

On the other side of the wall, separating the kitchen and the living room, stood a twelve-year-old boy who had come home in time to hear almost all of the conversation in the kitchen. About him. About the father he still dreamed of meeting. Since he was a little boy, he always wanted to know what he looked like. And he had heard about the Osage High School basketball team that won the state championship the year he was born. He didn't want to upset his mother, but he felt excited. And he was more than ready to meet his real father.

Chapter 14

Griffin left the house before anyone knew he was even there. He walked out to the unattached three-car garage to get his bike. It had been a long time since he had ridden that bike. It was a Christmas gift a year ago. One of the best road bikes money could buy. Lightweight, fast, and trendy, his father had boasted. Griffin needed that bike tonight because where he had to go was clear across town. Before he rode off, he texted his mother and told her he would be late for dinner. He lied and told her he and his best friend, Sam were doing homework with a girl he liked. Griffin knew he would have to answer a gazillion questions about that later, but it was okay. He did like Deonna Worley and he knew his mother was onto him anyway.

"Grif has a girlfriend," Lizzy said, after checking her cell phone when her son texted her. "She's going to make him late for dinner."

Gi giggled, and Kenzie commented, "Geez, he's twelve. The boy does take after Trey."

There was silence among them for a moment, and then Lizzy spoke. "What does he look like by now?"

"Damn good, actually," Kenzie admitted. "Even better than in high school. Less bulked up, I think. He's in great shape. His body actually is comparable to Peter's." God how she missed her husband. And yes, Trey's physique took her back to Peter for a moment when she recognized his body's resemblance.

"I still can't believe you both slept with the same guy," Gi interjected, attempting to break the solemn mood in that kitchen.

"He was my boyfriend," Kenzie stated, as a matter of fact, but she was long over what had once felt like a betrayal.

"I guess I wanted my cherry popped pretty badly," Lizzy teased and they all laughed.

"As badly as you wanted Hunky Hank in his apartment last time you saw him?" Gi laughed.

"Ugh. Let's not go there again," Lizzy begged, and both Kenzie and Gi laughed at her. They were, however, extremely proud of her for having the willpower to walk away from temptation.

"So will you talk to Max tonight before you tell Griffin about Trey being in town?" Kenzie inquired.

"I probably should," Lizzy replied, feeling skeptical, "but his reaction isn't going to be pretty."

"It's not his call to make," Gi spoke up. "Just be strong. And remember, this is for Griffin."

*

Griffin had known who his biological grandmother was, and where she lived in Lake Ozark. Lizzy never kept it a secret from him. He's always known his roots. The few times they had run into each other in public, and she looked away or pretended not to know him, Griffin was never hurt or angered by that. He had a family, two parents who wanted and loved him. Still, that never stopped him from being curious about what those people were like. Especially his real father.

Griffin laid his bicycle down on its side in the grass in the front yard of the white two-story house on the corner, where he was told his father grew up and his grandmother still lived. He walked up the uneven sidewalk, stepped up the three steps onto the front porch, and reached to ring the doorbell.

A moment later, he heard footsteps coming toward the door from inside. He held his breath when the door opened.

There stood a woman, maybe in her fifties. Tall. Thin. Slightly graying shoulder-length hair. She said *hello*, and after she added *may I help you*, her facial expression changed, and her eyes looked watery. She took two steps back. And then a man came from behind her.

Griffin stared at that man. Tall. Broad chest. Short dark hair. Physically fit.

"My name is Griffin," he felt brave as he spoke first. "You may know me as Lizzy Thomas' son." He used his mother's maiden name. As if they wouldn't know of her otherwise.

"Griffin…that's a great name." Trey had known what Lizzy had named her son. He just never had said his name out loud.

"Thank you," Griffin said to him.

"Please…come inside," the woman who was his paternal grandmother spoke, as she had regained her composure from the shock of Griffin just showing up. She had seen him before and known exactly what he looked like. His photograph was in the local newspaper all the time in the junior high sports section. *The apple had not fallen far from the tree,* Mrs. Toennies thought to herself many times.

Griffin stepped inside of the house and stood still again. He had never had a grandmother before. Kara Thomas died when his mother was in the first grade. And Max Zurliene's mother died soon after his parents were married. His mother told him he met her once, but Griffin was two years old then and did not remember.

"Mom, can I have some time here?" Griffin heard Trey ask his mother. She hesitated at first, because she truly wanted to stay. But then, she left the room and the two of them alone.

"Let's sit down," Trey suggested. His experience with high school-aged kids was going to be in his favor right now. But, he needed help with comprehending that this fine young man in front of him right now was his son. How could twelve years have gone by? And how could he have let it? Trey spoke first after they sat down, across the room from each other after both choosing tan suede chairs to sit down on versus a couch and loveseat.

"I am surprised you came to me so fast – and alone," Trey said.

"My mom doesn't know I'm here," Griffin stated. "I rode my bike."

"I see," Trey said, knowing he had pedaled a long way across town. He had already driven by the house Lizzy and her family lived in. And what a house it was. Lizzy had done well for herself and her son. "But your mother did tell you about me and how I wanted to meet you?"

"Not exactly," Griffin looked down to the floor as he answered him. "I overhead her with my aunts, Kenzie and Lizzy." Trey knew those women weren't blood-related to him, but it warmed his heart to know his son had grown up well-loved. "My mom said no. She didn't want me to see you. I took off before they saw me. I came here because I wanted to see what you're like. I always have."

Trey stared long at this boy, who was undoubtedly as wise as his mother. Lizzy had always been an old soul. And that night the two of them conceived a child, he had not seduced her. He was drawn to her and truly had felt connected. Lizzy had a way of reaching people, and so did her son.

Griffin was tall and hefty for his age. Trey could see he would mature just as he had. Early. Trey recalled clearly how he looked like a man when he still felt like a boy.

"I'm happy you came here. I think we have a lot to talk about. But in due time. I mean, I don't want to overwhelm you." Trey was being honest. He wanted more than a few-minute meeting with his son.

"So you're saying you didn't just want to meet me? Like maybe we could hang out sometime?" Griffin asked, and the way his eyes lit up and his lips curved into a slight smile made him look boyish. And Trey smiled.

"I would like that very much," Trey replied, "as long as it's okay with your mother."

Griffin nodded his head. "She may flip, but I think she'll understand. She's awesome like that."

"Then you're a lucky young man," Trey said, feeling like he was awfully lucky to get this chance today. And maybe it was just the beginning of life giving him a second chance.

"Can I ask you something?" Griffin asked.

"Anything," Trey replied.

"Don't you live in Boston?" Griffin inquired, because of what he overheard Kenzie tell his mother.

"I do. I teach and coach high school there," he told him.

"Then how will this work?" Griffin asked, gesturing in Trey's direction and then back at himself.

"I'll visit home more often...and maybe I could show you around Boston sometime? I have season tickets to the Celtics. We could see a game together?"

Griffin's eyes widened. At this moment he wasn't sure if he ever wanted to go home again.

✼

Lizzy had dinner ready when Max arrived home from work. His plate was full and his wine was poured when he sat down at the table.

"Looks great," Max said, eyeing the homemade chicken pot pie on his plate. "Where is Griffin and why aren't you eating with me?"

Lizzy stood with her back up against one of the stools near the island as Max sat at the head of their otherwise empty table. "Grif will be late, and I'm not hungry." She was holding a stemless glass of wine and she took a generous sip before continuing. "We need to talk."

Max was already shoveling forkfuls of his food into his mouth. His navy and red striped tie was loosened around his neck and the sleeves of his white dress shirt were rolled up to his elbows. She watched as his round stomach hit up against the table in front of him each time he leaned in for another bite off of his dinner plate.

"I heard today that Trey Toennies is in town, visiting his family," she began, and Max instantly looked up from his plate. "He reached out to Kenzie because he knows how close she and I still are. He wants to meet Griffin." Lizzy was careful not to say *his son*.

"I sure as hell hope you said no!" Max slammed his fork down on his plate and a loud clanging sound was heard in their quiet kitchen.

"Saying no was my initial reaction," Lizzy told him, and went after another swallow of her wine. She was looking for courage any way she could find it. "But I've decided to talk to Griffin. He's not a little boy anymore. He should know his biological father wants to meet him, and he should make this decision."

"Like hell!" Max retorted, as he stood up so abruptly from the table that his large stomach hanging over the belt on his suit pants, bumped the table and tipped over his wine glass. Lizzy immediately started to reach for the extra napkins on the table, but Max stopped her. "Leave it!" he said sternly. "You need to see this clearly. I am that boy's father. We are his parents, and we are a family. There is no room in Griffin's life for a loser daddy who fucked his mother once when he was just a horny teenager, and then abandoned him before he was even born!"

Lizzy inhaled a slow, deep breath. "This isn't for you to decide," she told him calmly.

"Do you see this place?" He threw up his hands in their kitchen with eighteen-foot-high ceilings. "I gave you both everything, you selfish bitch!"

Lizzy remained calm. This man, whoever he was, no longer had her honor and respect. She was trying to do the right thing for her son. She expected for this to possibly be the hardest on Max, given the fact that he was the adoptive father and only father Griffin had known all of his life. But what she never imagined was an attempt to be controlled in this verbally abusive manner. She had felt undeserving of many gifts from her husband over the years, but this type of treatment surpassed it all. She and her son did not deserve this.

Chapter 15

Gi walked into her house feeling happy to find her normalcy again. She was thinking how her life, compared to both Kenzie's and Lizzy's right now, didn't seem all that unbearable. She did miss her little girl as she had been with her much less lately. But, Ric had come through and was spending that time with their daughter.

Gi found both of them in the kitchen, eating take-out pizza for dinner. "Hey you two," she greeted them.

"Mommy, eat with us!" Suzie said, with pizza sauce on her little cheek.

"I think I will," Gi replied, sitting down across from Ric and next to their daughter. "Use your napkin, sweetie," she added, and then she made eye contact with her unusually quiet husband. "A pizza night, huh?" It was the second time this week.

"Don't be judgy, Gi. I've had three tow calls since I picked up Sooz from school." Ric was talking with his mouth full and Gi resisted the temptation to roll her eyes. It unnerved her though.

"At least you remembered to take our daughter along this time," she said in her typical snarky tone with him.

"Haha," he said, eating the last bite of the pizza on his plate. And then he stood up and walked his plate over to the dishwasher. "Now that you are home, I'm headed back to the shop."

"Oh? You're that busy?" Gi asked, finding his recent routine of returning to the shop a little odd. Not that she cared though, because she enjoyed having Suzie all to herself at nighttime.

"Yes, and I'm not complaining. The extra money is nice." Ric walked over to his little girl and kissed her on top of the head.

"Good night, daddy!" Suzie exclaimed, as if she knew he wouldn't be home in time to tuck her into bed later.

"Bye," Gi said, but Ric never looked back.

*

Gi layed beside Suzie in her twin bed, reading her a second book. When she closed that book, Suzie wasn't ready to sleep yet.

"Mommy? Tomorrow am I going to your store or with daddy to his shop again?"

"My store, if that's okay," Gi told her, knowing all too well she was a daddy's girl and enjoyed her time with Ric. That truth did make it easier for Gi when she needed to get away.

"Sure, it's okay, but I told Hollie I would see her tomorrow. I hope she won't think I'm a liar." Suzie looked genuinely concerned about that.

"Who's Hollie?" Gi asked.

"Daddy's right hand at the shop," she spoke confidently, repeating precisely what her daddy apparently had called Hollie.

"Oh, she must be his new receptionist?" Gi assumed. It had been at least six months since Ric's longtime secretary retired. That's how poor the conversation was between Gi and Ric. He never mentioned his new-hire, and Gi hadn't asked.

"She answers the phone and types really fast on the computer," Suzie spoke as a matter of fact.

"So does daddy leave you with Hollie sometimes?" Gi inquired.

"No, he's with us in there," she answered.

"Working?" Gi asked.

"Yeah, or just talking a lot," Suzie paused for a little while, and Gi could tell she was thinking about something. "She giggles at daddy. His jokes are funny."

"What does she look like?" Gi asked, feeling like she should be asking more about this Hollie. And maybe her questions needed to be addressed to her husband, not her little girl.

"She has hair like my Barbie doll," Suzie stated.

"Is she old and ugly with that pretty hair?" Gi asked, cracking a smile and Suzie giggled before answering her.

"No, you're silly mommy! She's right outta school." Now this was a five-year-old talking, so Gi needed to take that under consideration before she reacted to this. She considered a stop by the shop tomorrow to see for herself.

✱

Gi was still awake, lying in her own bed when Ric came home. She had been thinking for hours about what Suzie told her. It bothered her to no end. She scolded herself for letting this take over her thoughts. But, she had to know.

"You're really late tonight," she told him, as he acted as if he was on a mission to get a clean pair of boxer shorts out of the top dresser drawer and go straight into the master bathroom to shower.

"Busy, and just trying to stay ahead of the game for tomorrow," he stated, turning to look at her.

"How's Hollie working out for you?" There. She said it. She wasted no time getting right to what was on her mind. That was most definitely Gi's nature.

"Just fine," Ric answered, now knowing Suzie had been talking.

"That's good," she replied, as he stepped into the bathroom and closed the door. A minute later, Gi heard the shower water running.

Gi was wide awake when Ric slipped into their bed, wearing only boxers. She wore her usual oversized t-shirt and panties to bed. Those panties, however, were on the floor beside her bed right now. It had been a really long time since she let him touch her. She wasn't even sure if she wanted him to, but she was going to attempt to get his attention tonight. Because she needed to know something. *Was her husband doing more with Hollie than just making her giggle?*

Ric already had pulled the sheet and duvet up to his shoulders and turned his back to her. Gi moved closer to his bare skin, spooning her body with his. She lifted her t-shirt enough to move her leg over him. She took her hand and reached inside of his boxers. And that's where he met her hand with his. And moved it out of his pants. He had not been aroused. Yet.

"What are you doing?" he asked, not having moved his body. His back was still to her.

"I guess I need to remind you how this works," Gi told him as she moved him flat on his back and straddled him. He immediately realized she was panty-less, just as she pulled her t-shirt over her head and took it off. She was completely naked, straddling her husband and he froze.

She wanted to ask him to touch her, but should she really have to? She again reached into his pants. He didn't stop her that time. She moved down and took him into her mouth.

"Stop. Just stop, okay?" he said to her, as she looked up at him. And then she had her answer. She knew her husband was screwing his secretary.

"Why? You've begged me to do this before," she reminded him.

"I'm tired. I won't be able to."

"Are you getting it on with someone else? Are you cheating on me?" Gi stood naked alongside their bed, where Ric was still lying down.

Ric was silent before he answered. "I have needs, Gi. And you're not interested."

She swallowed hard. The sudden lump in her throat was building. "So now we live in an open marriage? I can go fuck someone too?"

"You do what you need to do, because I'm not who you want anymore," he made direct eye contact with her as he spoke and it dawned on her how long it's been since he had. It was as if the truth, his infidelity, being out in the open had freed him. *Why hadn't it done the same for her?* She used to wish she had a valid reason to kick him out of their marriage. But, for Suzie, she never made that move. *Or, was it really for herself?*

Chapter 16

As the sun was beginning to set, Kenzie's apartment was dark again. She didn't turn on a single light, and she kept the window blinds open because the feeling of being closed inside there, all alone, made her feel worse. Nights were the hardest for her.

She uncorked a bottle of wine in the kitchen, and brought both the bottle and a stemless glass in the living room with her. Her condo was spacious and comfortable. She and Peter had chosen all white furniture for the living room, and Kenzie was sitting in the middle of the sectional now. When her doorbell rang, it startled her as she poured more wine and spilled it over the side of the glass, splashing onto the coffee table. "Shit!" she said to herself as she stood up to see who was at the door. It was a little late for visitors, so Kenzie assumed Gi or Lizzy was there.

She made her way over to the door in her bare feet, faded flared denim with a hole in one knee, and a white t-shirt, sans a bra. She opened the door, and her eyes widened when she saw Trey Toennies standing there. She thought of her bra that she had taken off and flung onto her bed earlier. Kenzie crossed her arms over her chest, and spoke first. "Trey? Hi." She was surprised he knew where she lived.

"Hi, I'm sorry it's late. I was going to text you, but I just wanted to do this in person." Trey stood under the darkening sky. He too was wearing light-washed denim and a fitted red t-shirt. She didn't stare, but she thought he was wearing flip flips.

"It's fine, um, come in," she offered and stepped back. Her arms were away from her chest now and she just decided not to bother to cover herself. If she brought attention to trying, it would be obvious.

Kenzie quickly stepped ahead of him, and turned on two lamps, one on each end of the sectional. "Sorry, I like it dark when I'm alone," she told him, and that word *alone* echoed in her head. Trey had heard about Kenzie just getting married and her husband dying on their honeymoon. His mother told him about that tragedy when he told her that he met with Kenzie at her office. He had not known before.

"Wine?" she asked him, as he sat down on the end of the sectional, near one of the lamps.

"Yeah, sure, why not?" he answered. Her offer allowed him to assume she didn't mind him being there, or she had not hoped to rush him off. He needed someone to talk to tonight.

When Kenzie came back from the kitchen with a glass, Trey spoke first. "I heard about what happened to your husband, and I'm sorry for your loss."

"Yes, life has its moments and, for me, this one is a doozy. I don't quite know how I'll recover, to be honest," Kenzie spoke so freely with him. It had always been that way when they were just teenagers, and close friends before they dated.

"It sucks to be alone, I do know that," Trey told her.

"Missing your girlfriend, huh?" Kenzie asked, taking a generous swallow of her wine, and that reminded Trey he had yet to take a drink. He wasn't much of a wine drinker. He preferred beer, or even Scotch sometimes.

"I don't know if it's her I miss, or the idea of having someone to share it all with. Does that make sense or do I sound like an insensitive jerk?" he asked, with a lopsided grin. Kenzie had forgotten about that grin. It made her smile in return.

"No, I get you. It makes perfect sense. It also probably means you have not found *the one* yet. Because, take it from me, once you find her, she will be all you think about and compare every other woman to." Right now, Kenzie was thinking how – despite his darker hair – Trey reminded her of Peter. It was uncanny to her how similar their bodies were.

"Then I guess I haven't found her yet. And to be honest, after what happened tonight, I think looking for a woman is going to have to take a backseat in my life for awhile. I have someone else to focus on," he told her, and Kenzie shot him a curious look.

"My son…Griffin came to see me."

Kenzie's face dropped a bit. Her first thought was how incredibly fast that happened considering she had just left Lizzy's kitchen mere hours ago, and at that point Lizzy had not told Griffin or Max yet. "Did Lizzy bring him to you?"

"No. He came on his own after overhearing his mother talking about me with you and Gi," Trey informed her.

"Oh my," Kenzie reacted. "Lizzy is going to flip."

Trey smiled, "That's exactly what Griffin said."

"But she'll come around…" Kenzie added.

"That, too," Trey smiled.

"So what was it like to meet your son for the first time? I mean, I already know what an amazing kid he is, thanks to Lizzy." Trey expected that last jab.

"It was incredible," he smiled wide. "He looks like his mom, but he's gonna be built like me." Trey laughed, and Kenzie laughed harder.

"Are you sure, he's a chunky kid," she laughed again, thinking of Lizzy and how beautiful her fullness made her.

"Positive. He hasn't hit puberty yet. That'll do it," Trey chuckled again.

"I do remember you being slightly fuller than you are now. You look hot, by the way." It could have been the wine taking affect already, or possibly just the comfort of talking to an old boyfriend. "Seriously, you must work out like crazy. Peter did, and he saw results just like you."

Trey was flattered, and he also felt unbelievably comfortable with Kenzie. He had long forgotten how her direct honesty could keep a conversation going for hours. She had a way of reaching people, him too. And so it made perfect sense how she ended up a psychiatrist.

"I do work out, it's an obsession," he smiled. "I like how I feel, but even better I like what I see."

Kenzie giggled. "I get ya. I think it's important to love your own body, no matter what size you are really." Trey nodded his head. He wanted to tell her she still looked the same. *Both strikingly beautiful and sexy as hell.* "So, back to Grif. Did you make a good impression on my nephew?"

"I hope so, yeah, I think I did," Trey began. "I mean, he didn't at all appear to hold any ill feelings toward me. He said he's actually always wondered about me. We connected over basketball."

"Of course, you did," Kenzie smiled, as she poured herself another glass of wine, and Trey again realized he needed to drink his.

"Next, I hope to talk to Lizzy," Trey stated.

"And that's why you're here for me again?" Kenzie almost felt disappointed. She thought he just wanted to stop by to share his good news. But now, she assumed he only wanted her help again.

"No, not at all," he was quick to answer. "I honestly just wanted to talk to you. It's still easy, isn't it?"

"Yes, it is," Kenzie said, now knowing he too remembered *them*.

"Do you ever wonder what might have been?" he asked.

"If you hadn't slept with my best friend?" Kenzie was partly teasing. She was long over that.

"That too," he answered. "I think about that mistake and how my choice continued to snowball in my life." Kenzie knew he was referring to his commitment issues. "I took one look at him –at that boy who is my flesh and blood– and I knew I could not have been more wrong to turn my back on him."

"Yes, you were," Kenzie said to him. "But you're going to make it right now, and that's all that should matter."

"I hope Lizzy sees it like you do," Trey took a drink from his glass this time.

"Give her time to adjust," Kenzie said, believing that eventually she would.

"I'm sorry I hurt you that night," he brought it up. "Young and stupid."

"Grif wouldn't be here," she began. "That's how I very quickly learned to deal with what you and Lizzy both did."

"Thank you," Trey told her. "For not hating me forever. For going to Lizzy. Your actions indirectly already brought my son to me. I know that I want to be a part of his life."

"Now that is between you and his mother," Lizzy sat back on the sofa, still with her body turned toward him. There was one cushion separating them.

"It is. I'm hoping to talk to her tomorrow," Trey stated.

"Good luck," Kenzie said, raising her glass to him, which had barely a swallow of wine left in it, as Trey clinked his glass to hers.

"Thanks," he smiled, and watched her finish her second glass. "You're way ahead of me," he noted, still drinking the first glass she had poured for him.

"Yeah, I know, catch up, slow poke!" she laughed, and he smiled.

"So what was he like, your husband, I mean?" *Besides being one hell of a lucky man to have called this woman his wife,* Trey thought to himself as he eyed the multi-carat diamond ring she wore.

"Kind, funny, athletic, a little goofy, but very smart and successful," Kenzie spoke, not feeling as sad right now. She needed to remember Peter. And especially speak of him.

"You forgot lucky," Trey told her, and she gave him a confused look. *Lucky how? To have only lived to be thirty-two years old after receiving a horrible diagnosis?* "He found you. I know I would die a happy man."

"That's the worst come on I've ever heard!" she laughed at him.

"Well it wasn't meant to be one!" he laughed with her.

"So you are no longer attracted to me?" Kenzie teased him. She was tipsy, but she knew where she was going with this.

"I didn't imply that either," he told her, setting down his wine glass on the coffee table in front of them. She had already done the same. The last thing Trey wanted was to ruin this after they had been successful at resurrecting a lost friendship. "I should probably go."

"I'm sorry. I'm coming across as the needy, desperate widow," she admitted.

"Not at all," he told her. "I'm just trying not to fall head first into my old pattern with you.

Kenzie looked at him, sitting on the edge of the sofa cushion. "Which is?"

"Wanting to put my hands all over you." Their eyes locked. Trey knew he should leave now. Taking advantage of Kenzie while her grief for her husband was still so raw was crazy.

"No expectations. No analyzing this afterward. You go on back to Boston after your few days here, and I'll continue trying to get over my husband." Kenzie surprised herself, but not nearly as much as Trey. "I just need to feel close to someone. And after everything, after all the time that's passed, I trust you."

"I don't want you to regret this, because if you do – I will. And I have enough regret in my life." Trey wasn't looking for a way out. He didn't want an excuse to walk away from her tonight. He just didn't want to hurt her. She had suffered enough.

Kenzie moved onto the sofa cushion that was separating them. She made the first move. She initiated their kiss, and Trey was eager to respond. Their lips were familiar to each other. Only now they were experienced adults, well in tune with their bodies.

Trey was gentle with her. He knew her heart ached for her husband. He was well aware she could be thinking about him, missing *his touch*. But she had asked him to be there for her, to do this with her. He was an unattached twenty-nine-year-old man, he wasn't going to turn away from sex. But, more so, this was a girl he once loved. And could love her again as a woman.

Their kisses became deeper and more intense. The back of Trey's hand brushed against Kenzie's chest. Through her t-shirt, he had felt her nipple. It hadn't gone unnoticed to him earlier that she was not wearing a bra. He looked at her, with longing in his eyes. "It's okay, touch me, Trey. I won't break. I need this. I want you."

Trey took his hand and slowly slipped it up underneath her shirt. He felt the hardness of her nipple. She closed her eyes as he lifted up her shirt in the dim-lit living room. The lamps were allowing them to see just enough of each other. Her pink nipples tasted sweet between his lips.

She nearly tore off his shirt, unfastened his jeans. Her jeans and panties were now at her ankles. Trey moved his mouth between her legs. He found her pleasure spot and her moans begged him to show no mercy. A second after she came, Trey pushed himself inside of her. He was close to his climax. Kenzie remembered that look on his face all too well. She quickly moved from underneath him. He thought she wanted him to stop, that it was suddenly too much for her. But, she only wanted to be in control of this. She asked him to be with her tonight. He was flat on his back when she guided him inside of her. She gradually teased him at first with slow movements as she sat on his manhood. In and out. And then she rode him hard. When he exploded inside of her, he called out her name. And when she laid her head on his chest, tears were pooling in her eyes.

Chapter 17

Something that seriously annoyed Lizzy about her husband was how he could sleep unbelievably well following a serious fight with her. But, because Lizzy's mind was reeling and she had gone downstairs into the kitchen, she found Griffin ready to talk.

"I didn't want to tell you where I was tonight," he began, perched on the stool near the island in blue plaid pajama pants and a gray t-shirt. His thick, dark hair was still wet from the shower. And he had a tall glass of milk in front of him.

Lizzy pulled her favorite white fleece robe tighter over her chest as she sat down near her son. She wondered if they were about to have the sex talk.

"I came home from school today and you didn't know I was here," Griffin explained. "I overheard you with Kenzie and Gi. I know about my real dad being in town."

Lizzy covered her mouth with her hand. She had still been trying to work up the courage to tell him, despite Max's adamant objection. She couldn't believe Griffin had known the entire evening. "I'm sorry you had to find out like that. Be honest and tell me what your thoughts are about this. I'm going to let you decide, and I'll stand behind you no matter what, I promise."

"I went to him," Griffin told her. "I remembered the house you showed me across town, where Mrs. Toennies lives."

Lizzy gave her son a look that blared, *you've got to be kidding me!* And then she immediately spoke. "What happened?" she suddenly felt as if her son had grown up entirely too fast. He made an important, possibly life-changing, decision on his own today. And she wasn't there to be a part of it.

"We talked and it was really good," Griffin explained. "He's a teacher and a basketball coach in Boston." Lizzy could see the light in his eyes as he spoke of not just something random they shared in common, but *basketball*.

"How long will he be in town?" Lizzy knew she was next to see him.

"Just a few days, but he's coming back if you agree to it," he told his mother, completely rolling the ball into her court.

"What does he want me to agree with?" Lizzy held her breath.

"We both want a chance to get to know each other. Will you allow me to spend time with him? Like maybe even go to Boston to see the Celtics play?" Getting to know each other, spending time in Lake Ozark after Trey traveled *here* was one thought she was slowly getting used to, but her son going to Boston was so far from happening from Lizzy's viewpoint. She hoped Trey had not tried to bribe her son. Griffin has had enough extravagance in his lifetime. She was first now beginning to realize that. Lizzy thought of Max and what this might do to him once he found out Griffin wanted to be a part of his birth father's life.

"One moment at a time, Grif," she told him. "Give yourself a chance to process this. It's a huge change in your life. And I want you to be okay with it. If you're not, now or at any time, please talk to me."

Griffin nodded his head. "Just let me do this with him, to see where it goes. I know it sounds totally cheesy when I say this, but I already feel connected to him. I like him."

Lizzy pulled her son close. She didn't say anything else for a long while as she thought about how one night, twelve years ago with a teenage boy, had changed her world. She, to this day, did not truly know Trey Toennies. And she never concerned herself with that fact, because she didn't have to. Now, she was about to allow her son to get acquainted with his biological father. It was the right thing to do. But Lizzy was going to do it with her eyes wide open. It was still *her* responsibility to do what was best for her son.

※

"I need you to hear me out," Lizzy said to her husband as she walked into their bedroom to find him dressed for work, wearing all but his suit coat, which was lying neatly on the end of their bed. He looked at her in the mirror he was standing in front of, as he straightened another red tie. He always wore a red tie when he had to appear in court. He had told Lizzy over the years that it was power red for him, and always brought him great luck in courtroom.

"I talked to Grif last night," she began. "He actually brought this up to me. He overhead Kenz, Gi, and myself talking about Trey Toennies being in town. I didn't know this until last night, but Griffin went to see him on his own. He wanted to meet him."

Max slowly turned around from the full-length mirror in their bedroom. "You've got to be kidding me? He's a boy who's going to end up disappointed. I mean, really, what kind of person abandons their child? What could he possibly want with him now? He missed his entire childhood!"

"I know," Lizzy agreed, sitting down on the edge of their bed next to the neatly laid out suit coat. "Don't think I haven't thought about all that you are saying. I was the girl who was pregnant and scared to death. I was most affected by Trey's decision to walk way. I was the only parent Griffin knew from the time he has born to two years later when you came into our lives. But, because our son has had a great upbringing with us, he's a good boy. He does not hold any hate in his heart. He doesn't have a grudge against Trey for not being in his life. He does, however, want to get to know him." Lizzy was really trying to reach Max, but he threw up his hands into the air. "We must allow him to do this. And we will be there to pick up the pieces if we have to." Lizzy continued to speak of them as a couple, as Griffin's parents. She had no idea what was going to happen to her marriage, or if she truly wanted to save it. Right now, she was only trying to save Max's relationship with Griffin. She wanted Max to see that nothing had to change between them.

"So what happens next?" Max asked his wife, as he picked up his suit coat from the bed, near her.

"I have to meet with Trey," she answered, "and don't think -after all these years and given our circumstance- that will not be awkward."

"I'm going to look into this further. Legally, we can keep him from having rights to Griffin. A couple of visits, sure, have at it. Then get the fuck out of our lives." Max now had both of his arms shoved into his suit coat, and he was barely able to fasten the middle button in the front. His round stomach was protruding above and underneath it.

"You're not hearing me. That is not for us to decide. It's Griffin's life." Lizzy was adamant, and Max was angry.

"He's my son!" were the last words Max had screamed at her before barreling out of their bedroom and slamming the door behind him.

✻

Lizzy had Trey's cell phone number logged into her phone. Kenzie had given it to her. He was expecting Lizzy to contact him. He was only in town for a few days, she had heard from more than one person. It was time to reach out.

The convenience of sending a text message was not having to speak to him. Right now, Lizzy's nerves had taken over and she believed her voice wouldn't even work properly. It would be shaky, at best.

The text she sent to him was simple and to the point. *I would like to meet you for coffee this morning. Starbucks at 8:30?* Not even one minute later, Lizzy received her response from Trey. *I'll be there.*

Lizzy drove to Osage Beach Parkway. She didn't know if she had arrived first. She was ten minutes early, so she just went directly inside to order herself a coffee and find a table or a booth. Preferably one in a private corner. It's not as if she was meeting a friend for a social visit.

She ordered a dark roasted espresso, and turned to scan the seating area. Back in a far corner, she saw a man who could have been him. His hair was shorter, his shoulders were still broad. Lizzy remembered Kenzie saying *he looked smaller, but he was still hot.* It was him, Lizzy was sure of it when he waved her over as he stood up from where he sat.

Lizzy felt her own heartbeat quicken as she took the steps over toward him. She clenched the strap on her handbag with her free hand. And then she was there, standing right in front of the man who she gave her virginity to, and he left her with a baby boy.

"Liz, hi," he said first, and he had shortened her name. *He knew she was still called Lizzy, but she was a woman now, a far cry from the teenager he had connected with at a party, a party where his girlfriend had just been one floor under them while he had taken another girl to bed.*

"Hi Trey," she managed to respond without choking on her own saliva.

"Let's sit," he offered, and when she placed her coffee on the table, she noticed he had ordered a green tea. *Of course. With a body like that, a sip of coffee wouldn't be a part of the equation.*

Lizzy pushed her handbag further down on the seat as she sat in the middle, facing a man who was possibly going to be suddenly intertwined into her life, because of *their* son.

Trey spoke first. "I know this is awkward," he admitted, and Lizzy thought how he hadn't changed. He had a way about him to make everyone feel comfortable by just saying how he felt. "I want to thank you for meeting with me. You could have so easily blown me off. I'm undeserving of this chance, I know that, but I want this so badly. I guess what I'm trying to say is, you could have told me that I'm twelve years too late. But, you didn't. You're here."

Lizzy shifted her body weight in the booth across from him. She felt uncomfortable. Her jeans were a little snug around the waist and the skin on her soft stomach felt pinchy in them. She tried harder to focus on what he was saying, but this was difficult for her.

"I'm here," she said, "because of my son. I think you know that he wanted to see you. If he hadn't, I would have respected his decision. From the time he was old enough to understand, I told him he was adopted by my husband, the man he has called *dad* since he was two years old. When he asked where his *real dad* was, I told him that you were not ready to be a father when he was born. And I left it at that. I have never bad-mouthed you. To be honest, I've never given you too much thought. I just learned to be there for my son, and then when I got married so many of my worries and all of my fears just diminished. My top priority was to make a good life for my son." Lizzy left out the fact that she never loved her husband and marrying him was not about her. It was stability and financial security for her son. Lizzy was finally mature enough to admit that to herself now.

"I commend you for all you've done, your husband too," Trey added. He didn't know much about Max Zurliene, only that he was a successful attorney in the Lake Ozark and Osage Beach area. Driving by their home had awed him, too. Teaching and coaching in Boston was a far cry from the life Lizzy was living with his son.

"Thank you," Lizzy responded.

"I want to explain something to you," he stated. "When I met Griffin, regret flashed before my eyes like it never had. And I've thought and dwelled on this a lot. But, this time, seeing him, talking to him, studying his face, his hands, his gait, all of it – made me want more. I missed it all, I know that. I was a loser and a coward, and I had my mother's support to run from my mistake."

"Griffin was not a mistake," Lizzy chimed in.

"No, he wasn't. But until I met him –a living, breathing being, who I helped create– I had no idea." Trey sighed, and took a long sip of his green tea that just looking at had turned Lizzy's stomach. "He's an amazing kid."

"Yes, he is. Take the time to get to know him, and you'll be further awed. Just don't use him to make yourself feel better about your mistake. Don't bribe him. Be real with him. Because if you aren't, he will see through you." Lizzy felt stronger at this moment than she had when she first walked up to this man. Her son always brought her strength when she needed it most.

"I will," Trey nodded his head repeatedly. "This time, I won't screw up. I promise you that, Lizzy."

Chapter 18

It had only been three days since Gi found out Ric was having an affair. She knew their marriage had been repeatedly taped and glued back together after they fell out of love – but their focus had always been on Suzie.

Suzie was at school, and they were home alone. Ric had gone upstairs for the last of his things. Just clothes, shoes, and necessities. That's all he wanted to take with him. Gi could have the house, he had already decided. That would provide stability for their little girl, living there with her mother. Part of the time. She would also stay with him. He rented an apartment. And his girlfriend had already moved in. She was waiting for him there now, as Ric was saying goodbye to his wife, their marriage, and their life together that had not been healthy for either of them for a very long time.

Gi stood in front of the television in the living room. She had a cup of coffee in her hand, which she added a shot of vodka to a few minutes ago in the kitchen. She needed a little help getting through this day. Standing there, the television flashed in front of her eyes. There was a time when the console set, on the shag-carpeted flooring in that old rundown trailer she grew up in, was the only thing she had to keep her company. To keep her mind off of how sad she was. Gi instantly turned off the television. Just the memory of it now ticked her off. She was way better than that now. She no longer was that frightened little girl who had to act tough. Or was she? As a woman, she still fought those demons. From the moment her marriage began to lose the love, Gi had been on the defense with Ric. He could never do anything right. Except for being a good father, and even with that, she always found faults to criticize him for. And he, in turn, could be an asshole. They fought like crazy, but that too was coming to an end. They had already agreed to share their daughter and to never put her in the middle of any of their issues.

Ric came down the steps, in his work boots, jeans, and fitted navy blue t-shirt. His hair looked gelled today, and Gi wondered if he was going to work. *He never styled his hair for work.* She stood there feeling a lot less put together in her burnt orange t-shirt, black leggings, and bare feet. Her hair was untouched this morning, and hanging in her eyes more than usual. She tucked it back behind her ear as she turned away from the dark screen on the television and looked at him from across the room where she remained still.

"I think I have everything," he told her, setting an open-lid cardboard box down on the hardwood floor at his feet.

"If not, you'll see Suzie on Tuesday, right? You can get whatever you need then." Gi was being civil because she was downright sad. The anger was surprisingly gone. *Yes, he was unfaithful. But, she knew he wasn't the only loser in this marriage to blame.*

"Okay, sounds good," Ric spoke as if they were making plans for dinner. "Um, we can still FaceTime before bedtime every night right?" They had agreed no matter who Suzie was with at nighttime, when it was time for bed and for her to say prayers, they both still wanted to be present. And technology could make that possible.

"Of course," Gi nodded. "Sooz will love that." Gi hadn't told her about their plan. So far, Suzie had handled the news of her parents living in separate houses very well. Gi had been taken aback when she and Ric told her the news together, and their daughter had asked if Hollie was going to live at her daddy's new place. It was as if Gi had been sucker punched in the stomach. For a long moment, she had struggled to take a breath. And then it dawned on her that Ric could be happy with another woman. Happier than he was with her. And possibly his newfound happiness would allow Suzie to be a part of a healthy, happy environment where two people could make each other laugh. Gi recognized her faults, and Ric's too. They were both to blame. And now, as they moved on from each other, their main concern was still their daughter. Suzie was going to be just fine.

"I should go then," Ric said, bending forward to pick up the box again at his feet. Gi swallowed hard, but it didn't prevent that lump in her throat from swelling.

He stopped and turned around after he took three steps toward the door. "Don't forget to turn the AC back at night, and the bathroom sink does have a leak. I'll take a look at it soon, when I get a break in my schedule. I can stop by when you're working at the store or something."

"Alright," she said, wondering why she had never realized all he did for that old house that they had yet to *fix up* together. Ric made it all the way to the door. He shifted the box to one arm and reached for the doorknob with his free hand.

"If you ever need a tow, I know a guy," he said, looking back at her. His eye contact pierced through her. Gosh it had been so long since they really looked at each other. And truly heard what the other was saying.

Gi smiled. "I wouldn't call anyone else," she was able to say without choking up.

Ric nodded his head and smiled. And then he was gone. The door was closed between them.

And that's when Gi fell to her knees. There was a nail head on one of the slabs in the hardwood that needed to be flattened with a hammer. Her knee hit that edge just so, and finally Gi freed those tears. Maybe her knee pained her. Or perhaps it wasn't that at all. Something sure as hell was ripping her apart right now.

Chapter 19

Kenzie was sitting behind her desk in her sixth floor office at the hospital. She was in-between patients and should have been reviewing the file for her next appointment. But her mind kept going there.

She had not answered the text Trey sent the morning after. *I would like to see you again before I leave for Boston.*

Kenzie had not responded for more than one reason. She knew Trey needed to focus on his son. And also because she was not interested in nurturing a romantic relationship. It was more than too soon. *She and Trey had amazing sex. That's all it was.*

Just as she was about to force her mind on work, her cell phone buzzed. She reached for it on her desktop. The message was from Gi and sent to both her and Lizzy. *I need you two. I'm getting a divorce.*

That was the first Kenzie had heard of this. She immediately responded. *I'll be there. Time and place?* And right then a reply from Lizzy came through. *Oh dear God. Where are you now?*

While both Kenzie and Lizzy awaited some direction from Gi, Kenzie picked up her desk phone and told Alisa to cancel her last three appointments for the afternoon because she had an emergency.

*

Kenzie was standing outside of her car, parked along the street in front of Gi's house. She quickly took off her white lab coat that she had forgotten to leave hanging on the back of her chair in her office before she rushed out. Just as Kenzie threw the coat onto her passenger seat, Lizzy was pulling up behind her in that brand new black Escalade.

They rushed to each other on the street. "I had no idea," Lizzy spoke first, "I mean I'm not shocked because there's no love lost there, but I thought they were in this for Suzie."

"You're as clueless about this as I am right now," Kenzie told her. "Let's go inside."

Gi met them at the door as they stepped onto her front porch. The hunter green paint was peeling on the wooden floor boards at their feet. Gi momentarily thought about all of the repairs left undone.

"Come in you two," she said, relieved to have them there. She hesitated to reach out, but she needed them. And the three of them had never failed each other throughout all of their lives together.

They all three sat on the beige sofa in the living room. The television was off. The blinds were closed. And there was an empty glass mug on the coffee table with a half-full bottle of blueberry vodka beside it. Kenzie recognized the coffee table drinking. She had done that more than once since she returned to her condo alone.

"Tell us what happened," Lizzy said, rubbing Gi's knee, as she sat between them.

Without crying, Gi immediately began to explain. "I found out Ric was having an affair."

"Who with and for how long?" Lizzy asked, and Kenzie chimed in, "You finally had your reason to kick him out."

Gi took her time answering their questions. "I found out from Suzie of all people. It seems that her time spent with daddy at the shop after school also included Hollie, Ric's new secretary. She apparently makes daddy happy, and daddy makes the girl who looks like a Barbie doll, laugh a lot. I confronted him, but you'll never guess how," Gi stated, and then answered for them. "I came onto him, seriously willing to give him a blowjob or the best sex we hadn't had in forever. And he turned me down. He had gotten home late from work. I knew then he had been with another woman. I asked, he admitted it."

"Oh honey," Lizzy said to her and Kenzie watched Gi's expression change.

"I didn't kick him out. He never gave me a chance to," Gi told them. "He wanted to leave, he wants a divorce. He has a life waiting for him, and it doesn't involve me anymore."

"Bastard," Kenzie said, feeling sickened for what her best friend was going through.

"Yeah, that's what I thought too, at first," Gi spoke, "but I'm not angry. I'm really hurt though. I'm in so much pain, I can't hardly stand it. I thought I would be the one to leave. I've wanted to for years. We stopped talking, but kept on fighting with each other. And then he gave up. I'm left reeling and I don't even know why. Can't I just be relieved he's gone? I've always wanted to be free of him."

"Maybe you loved him more than you realized?" Lizzy carefully offered her opinion.

"I know how you hate when I bring up my patients, but I've seen cases like this," Kenzie stated. "We all get really comfortable just living, even if the day-to-day motions make us angry or sad or only in love with the people around us part of the time, we still become accustomed to that being our life. And those people in it, good or bad, become a part of us. You're grieving for your husband. Not at all the same way I am, but even still you are missing him and your heart is broken for what will never be again."

Gi put her face in her hands and began to cry. Both Kenzie and Lizzy leaned in to her and held her. As it always happened, when one of them cried, they all three did.

It took Gi awhile to regain her composure, closely sandwiched between them on the sofa, but when she did, she had something else to say. "I'm so afraid that I don't know who I am without some form of craziness in my life. It's always followed me. From growing up with my mother to living with Ric. I have had to be rigid to survive. With Ric gone, I don't have a reason to fight. Is that sickening or what? Being on the defense was how I've always lived."

"You are wrong," Kenzie said, as Lizzy looked at her with wide eyes. She didn't know what to say, and had hoped the psychiatrist among them would come through. "Your strength, from the moment I met you in kindergarten, inspired me. Yes, you've had to fight to keep your head above the water too many times, but you've never let that completely define you. You are amazing at running a business. And even better, the kind of mother you are to little Suzie is selfless and loving and she adores you beyond words. You are going to be just fine. Even better," Kenzie added.

Gi again was crying. "Ugh, I need to focus on you two right now. It's what we do best. Tell me about the latest."

"I met with Trey Toennies this morning," Lizzy blurted out. "The last time I saw him was right after I found out I was pregnant with Grif. Talk about an uncomfortable feeling." As Lizzy spoke, Kenzie wondered if she should tell them what happened between her and Trey. *Would they even understand?*

"Are you going to allow Griffin to at least meet him?" Gi asked, now feeling better as she focused on someone else.

"He already did. He left the house after overhearing us three in the kitchen. He took his bike to the Toennies house."

"Holy shit, was the wicked witch of the west home?" Kenzie asked, and they all giggled.

"He met her, too, but it was brief," Lizzy stated.

"If you ask me, that woman has looked like she's carrying some serious guilt for years now," Kenzie noted.

"I hope she is," Lizzy replied, knowing Trey's mother had taken charge and pushed him to be a free college kid, not to be tied down as a father at eighteen years old. "Griffin already likes Trey. We all three know how he so easily reels people in. I guess that's a good quality, if you use it honestly."

As Lizzy spoke, Gi laughed out loud. "Count me out of that *we!* I'm one of three here who didn't drop her panties for him." Kenzie stared down at the floor for a moment and she flashed back in her mind to her own panties at her ankles just a few nights ago.

"I told Griffin that he can take the reins, but I will be right behind him if he needs me. And I told, well no, I warned Trey not to hurt my son."

"It sounds to me like Trey and Griffin are going to be okay. I mean, if you're prepared to share him. That's what this will come to if they enjoy getting to know each other." Kenzie wanted to be sure that Lizzy was ready for that.

"I'm not okay with that from my own standpoint," Lizzy said, "but I have to learn to accept it for Grif's sake. He has a right to get to know his father. And Trey has very serious regret. I know he was being genuine when he told me that. Don't you think so, Kenz?"

"Why are you asking me?" Kenzie was immediately on the defense, and both Gi and Lizzy noticed.

"Well if you don't trust him, or believe that he wants to make a positive change in his life, why would you have come to me on his behalf?" Lizzy suddenly felt miffed.

"I do believe that, of course I do. He was my boyfriend for several months and we were close friends first, back then. He's a good person," Kenzie tried to explain herself, stressing their past relationship.

"If you both see good in him, I think we have to sit back, watch this play out for Griffin, and just support him," Gi said, realizing Lizzy was concerned about something more.

"It's Max who's going to get in the way," Lizzy admitted, shaking her head. "He keeps reminding me that Trey made a choice and he should be forced to live with it. No second chances. I think he reminded me twenty times in two days how *he is Griffin's father*.

"You can't blame him for feeling a little left out," Gi defended Max.

"But he doesn't have to be an asshole about getting his feelings hurt," Kenzie stated as a matter of fact.

"I don't know what is going to happen yet," Lizzy said, "but Max isn't the man I thought I married. He's been really mean and ornery about this."

"I think the Hank thing, prior to this, didn't help," Gi said.

"He has been more controlling than usual since then, yes," Lizzy agreed. She had not seen Hank since the night she left his apartment with mixed feelings.

"With you or Griffin?" Kenzie asked.

"Me. He's overdosing on Viagra almost nightly," Lizzy rolled her eyes, and both Kenzie and Gi were instantly sickened by the image of it.

"Is he forcing you to have sex with him?" Gi asked, feeling terrible for Lizzy.

"I'm obliging," Lizzy answered, "but I hate him a little more each time."

"Leave him," Kenzie blurted out.

"He's going out of town next week for business, and that's when I have an appointment with an attorney. The guy is the one in Osage Beach that Max has mentioned more than a few times. He's his rival in the courtroom. Max has lost to him three times this year alone."

"Smart woman," Gi said to Lizzy, as Kenzie reached overtop Gi's lap to take Lizzy's hand.

Chapter 20

The night before Trey was going back to his home in Boston, he had asked Lizzy's permission to have dinner with Griffin.

Before Max was due home from court, both Lizzy and her son were waiting for Trey to arrive. He drove up their driveway right on time, and Griffin seemed excited. "Should I just run out, or do you want to have him come inside?" he asked his mother.

"It's polite to invite him in for a minute," Lizzy told him, as she was trying very hard not to be nervous about this. Griffin obviously wasn't the least bit tense.

Griffin met Trey at the door before he rang the bell. When he opened the door, he told Trey he was ready, but his mom wanted him to come inside for a minute. Lizzy laughed to herself at how her son didn't yet know the first thing about being subtle.

"Hi," Lizzy said, as Trey stepped inside.

"Hello, you sure have a beautiful home," Trey said, looking up at the eighteen-foot ceiling in the foyer.

"Thank you," Lizzy responded. "So, Grif tells me you two are headed out for burgers and basketball?" Lizzy was used to seeing her son in long, oversized athletic shorts. It was Trey she looked twice at now. He was wearing black athletic shorts and a charcoal gray t-shirt, and matching charcoal gray tennis shoes. Even in comfortable clothes, he looked extremely fit.

"Yes, we are focused on fun tonight," Trey responded, smiling at their son first, and then at Lizzy.

"Fun? It won't be fun when I whoop you on the court!" Griffin teased, and Trey's face lit up like Lizzy had never seen. *Genuine*, she thought, as she watched the two of them share playful banter, back and forth. And then she heard footsteps behind her. She turned to find Max was home early.

"Hello," he spoke, and his voice sounded deeper.

"Hi Dad," Griffin spoke to Max first. "Um, this is my, this is–"

"I'm Trey Toennies," Trey said, finishing Griffin's sentence and reaching for Max's hand.

"Max Zurliene, Lizzy's husband and Griffin's father," he spoke, firmly shaking Trey's hand.

"You have quite a home here," Trey said to him, trying, really trying to keep things civil with a man who acted as if he wanted to instigate something more.

"That we do," Max replied. "Hard work pays off. A man who can provide for his family in spades is a success."

"I agree," Trey said, holding his own. *This guy was a piece of work.*

"Griffin is going out for bite to eat," Lizzy said, prompting Max to politely allow them to leave.

"I see," Max spoke, not taking his eyes off of Trey. "Well, enjoy, and I'll see you later, son." Griffin nearly bounced out of the door as he told them goodbye, and Trey followed him.

The car had not been backed off the driveway yet, and Max was already ranting. "You didn't tell me our son had plans with him tonight? I was under the impression that he had already left town and gone back to Boston for good!"

"This is his last night here," Lizzy said, hoping that statement would appease him.

"He looks like a kid himself, I mean, did you see the way he was dressed?" Max criticized.

"They are going out to play basketball after they eat burgers," Lizzy defended.

"You allowed our son to make those plans without consulting me first?" Max asked her while they continued to stand in the foyer.

"This is Griffin's call. Not mine. And not yours. I told you as his mother I am going to allow this. I'm here if I need to step in, but honestly I don't feel like it's my place. Or yours." Lizzy was feeling bold about this, and she was tired of Max's adamancy about it.

"I raised that boy as my own," Max said, loosening his tie and unbuttoning the first two buttons on his white dress shirt. "I have a say so. And I say after tonight, Trey Toennies should stay in Boston for good."

"That's not our call to make," she spoke sternly, and then she turned to walk up the long staircase. The first level above the stairs reached Max's bedroom, and a Jack and Jill bathroom that led to another living area and a game room. The level above that floor was the bedroom and master bathroom she shared with Max. They also had a third living area, and a workout room on that floor, which neither of them utilized.

"Don't walk away from me!" he demanded as he picked up his pace to follow her up the stairway. "I told you that Max is mine, and I will legally fight both you and his daddy-wanna-be!" Max was screaming and Lizzy kept climbing the stairs in front of him. He started to take two steps at a time to catch up to her.

They reached the first landing and Lizzy was prepared to keep walking, but Max was able to reach her and he grabbed her arm with a force that spun her around. "Don't," he warned her. "You are not equipped with the brains or the power to fight me." Those were extremely hurtful words for Lizzy to hear. *There were countless times when she had wanted to continue her education after they were married, but Max had talked her out of it. She belonged in their home, raising their son.*

"I am his mother, that's all the power I need," she spat those words at him. She would not let him see her fear.

"And you are also my wife," he said, not releasing her from his grip.

"You are hurting me," she said, trying to wiggle from his grip, but it hurt too badly. He was bruising her arm just above the elbow. She could already see the discoloration on her skin.

"As I said, you are my wife." Lizzy didn't like the look she saw in his eyes. He was going to force her to be submissive to his desires again. He released her arm and she stood in front of him and watched him undo his pants. "I've always fantasized about getting a blowjob on this stairway…"

Oh my God, no. She was sickened by his abuse. The power he held over her to pleasure him had gone too far. He had never been like that in their marriage before. She hated it. She hated him.

He dropped his suit pants and then pulled down his boxer shorts just far enough to reveal his erect manhood. "On your knees, my loving, obedient wife." This wasn't who she was. Lizzy Thomas was stronger than that. And if her husband believed otherwise, he was going to be sorely disappointed.

She watched him touch himself first. "Go on," he told her again. And this time, Lizzy moved to her knees on the landing directly in front of the stairway. She inched closer to him, putting both of her hands on his manhood, then she shoved him with all of her strength. And her husband lost his balance and fell backwards all the way down to the bottom of the stairs.

In a moment of fear and desperation, she took a chance. Max could have only broken a bone or two. Or worse.

His body lay bent and still. And his neck was awkwardly cocked to one side. She didn't hesitate for a second to call for emergency help after he fell down the stairway. And while she waited for the ambulance, she pulled up and refastened her husband's pants.

Chapter 21

Lizzy sat in her lawyer's office in Osage Beach. *Daryl Brokering, Attorney at Law,* was engraved on a name plate at the edge of his desk. She knew of him only from what her husband had said over the years. He was a fierce divorce attorney. A man with a wide infectious smile. He cared about people, but he cared more about winning. Little did she know that he was the man her husband had hired to be his own private attorney, in the event of his death. And for the reading of his will.

Lizzy sat beside Griffin as they listened to her husband's words being read to them. Max Zurliene's estate was worth twelve point five million dollars. He left everything he owned to his wife, and a special savings account had been in place for his son, Griffin Thomas Zurliene, for when he turned twenty-one years old.

Tears were pooling in Griffin's eyes. His father was dead. How ironic that the night he was getting to know his birth father, his adoptive father tragically died. Griffin didn't understand how he could have fallen. He had seen him barrel up and down those stairs thousands of times. He also didn't understand how his mother had been holding herself together. *Was she really that strong?* Lizzy broke down at the funeral, but she wasn't as devastated as a wife who had just lost her husband should be. Griffin had witnessed his Aunt Kenzie's sadness in recent weeks. He expected a little of the same from his mother. But, she had yet to show much emotion at all.

When Lizzy and her son left the attorney's office, she knew she was financially set for life, as was her son. Her gratitude for Max Zurliene would last forever, but she couldn't deny how there was a part of her that felt more than relieved the son of a bitch was gone.

Griffin went for a drive with Trey. He had delayed his plans to return to Boston until after the funeral. Trey chose not at attend though, believing it wasn't appropriate for him to be there. He did, however, offer endless support to both Griffin and his mother.

Lizzy was not alone when Griffin left. Both Kenzie and Gi were by her side, and had been for days. They, too, recognized Lizzy's reaction to her husband's death. Unlike Griffin though, they knew the truth. And they were the only ones who knew.

Lizzy told them everything that had happened, leading right up to when she pushed Max and he fell backwards down the stairs. Both Kenzie and Gi supported Lizzy to no end, but they had been afraid for her.

She relayed *her* story to the police detectives. She played the part of a shocked, distraught wife, who had witnessed her husband accidentally fall down the stairs. And the case was closed. There was no reason to further investigate that tragic accident. The late Max Zurliene was an upstanding citizen. A well-respected business man. A pillar in the community with a wife and son he adored. Sadly, their perfect family was no more. That's how the community of Lake Ozark perceived them.

"How are you holding up?" Gi asked, as Kenzie stood near the island, pouring wine in all three of their glasses.

"Still in disbelief," Lizzy responded, taking the first glass Kenzie had just filled.

"That's understandable, drink up," Gi told her, as Kenzie sat down alongside of them.

"Griffin can never know," Lizzy spoke quietly, even though she knew for certain he and Trey were driving around Lake Ozark, or possibly playing a game of one on one at the schoolyard.

"He won't," Kenzie assured her, "and he will be just fine. You will, too. You just need to figure out a way to forget."

"Like that's possible," Lizzy spoke, letting out a sigh. "I didn't plan for it to happen, but for a split second I wanted him dead, and I reacted to that. How awful is that?"

"He was awful to you," Gi defended her. "In a way, it was self defense on your part."

"Just focus on moving on with your life," Kenzie told Lizzy. "You're free, you definitely have the means to do what you want. I say go for it. Maybe call up Hank Stewart?"

"Don't think I haven't thought of that," Lizzy instantly replied. "It was thoughtful of him to come to the funeral."

"Did you talk to him?" Gi asked.

"Very little. He offered his condolences and we hugged – but so did everyone else."

"Was it a tight body-to-body hug, where you could feel his firm pecks or maybe the bulge in his pants?" Gi asked, giggling.

"I didn't think that intently about it as it was happening," Lizzy grinned. "There were people around. And besides, I rejected him. I'm sure he's long over me."

"Just give this all some time," Kenzie advised her. "You're young, with your whole life ahead of you. Trey coming into your son's life right at this time has to be a godsend."

"I know, I've thought exactly that," Lizzy spoke again. "I even wondered, and you're both going to think I'm crazy… but what if it could work between Trey and I?" No one said a word. Gi thought it was a bad idea. They had nothing in common except for the son they conceived at an under-aged drinking party over a dozen years ago. Kenzie caught her breath, and immediately reached for her wine glass. She could not say why the mere thought of that bothered her.

Gi spoke first. "Do not go there. Think of your son. He needs this relationship to work between him and his biological father. You do not need to risk making things more awkward with Trey Toennies in your life. Seriously, do not complicate it. You have a clean slate. Enjoy it. Spend money. Get laid with no expectations."

As Gi rambled, Kenzie tensed up. *Is that what she did with Trey? If it was casual sex, why did it bother her to know Lizzy could be interested in pursuing a relationship with him? So what if he fathered her child when she was a teenager! Kenzie wanted to tell Lizzy to leave this the hell alone.*

*

Almost an hour later, the girls were sharing their second bottle of wine when Griffin came home, and Trey walked him inside.

Kenzie sat up a little straighter on her stool, and didn't make eye contact with him at first. Griffin was talking, so she stayed focused on him after Lizzy asked why they were back so soon, and he answered that Trey had an early flight back to Boston in the morning.

Trey looked at Kenzie and probably stared longer than he should have. This was the first time they saw each other since the night they had sex on her living room sofa. Kenzie caught his eye, and then quickly looked away.

"Thank you for staying a few more days, I know you need to get back to teaching," Lizzy said to Trey as she got off of her stool, and walked over to him and their son.

"It's okay, it wasn't problem at all," Trey said, and Kenzie watched him reach out and squeeze Lizzy's hand. And it obviously bothered Kenzie as she grabbed her wine glass and took a long swallow.

"Well, I appreciate your support – we both do," Lizzy said, looking at her son. It was obvious how caught up Griffin already was with Trey.

"I'm going to head out," Gi said, breaking up their party. "I have to pick up Suzie at her dad's in less than ten minutes." The girls said a brief goodbye, and Gi was gone.

"I should go, too," Kenzie said, wanting to bolt out of that kitchen, and she wished she had spoken up earlier.

Kenzie hugged Lizzy, kissed Griffin on the cheek, and before she was going to wave at Trey and say something along of the lines of *have a safe trip back home*, he spoke first.

"Wait up, I'll walk you out." Kenzie froze. She watched Griffin hug Trey. She heard Trey promise his son they would talk daily, and he would let him know the next time he could fly home for a visit.

Lizzy backed up as the two of them said their goodbye. Trey reached out and again squeezed Lizzy's hand. "Be safe," Lizzy spoke, and then Kenzie felt him following her out of the door.

She picked up her pace on the windy sidewalk in front of the house. The landscape lights illuminated her path. "Hey, wait up," Trey said, reaching her side.

"I don't want it to be awkward between us," Kenzie spoke first.

"It doesn't have to be," he told her, as she continued to walk to her car and then she noticed he was parked behind her on the driveway, blocking her in. "I was just hoping to get a response to my text. Instead, you ignored it." Trey called her out.

"I did," she admitted, "because my life is so unbalanced right now. I don't know if I'm coming or going on most days. I'm just barely keeping my head above the water. Why would I want to drag you –or anyone– into that?"

"I can swim," Trey answered, and he smiled at her. Kenzie unwillingly found herself reciprocating that warm smile.

"I know, I remember," she laughed. Her first time skinny dipping in Lake Ozark had been with Trey. He had talked her into losing her bikini when they jumped off of his uncle's pontoon boat and swam off together in the darkness. They were close to shore, but afterward it had taken Trey forever to find both pieces of her swimsuit in the sand, while she waited in the water, impatiently giggling.

She smiled at the memory, and Trey spoke again. "I have to go back to Boston, but it's not going to be forever. I now have a reason to come back here."

"Yes, you do. Your son needs you more than ever. Be there for him," Kenzie stressed.

"I will," Trey assured her. "I also would like to be with you, to help you through your sadness."

"I can't," Kenzie said, as she reached her car door and had already used the remote control start to turn over the engine.

Trey put his hand on her car door, preventing her from opening it. "You and I have something here."

"I have a husband that I need to get over," she didn't like how those words came out, but she felt flustered and sort of meant what she said.

"No," Trey told her, standing close, with his hand still firmly pressed against the car door. "We don't get over our great loves. We just find a way to tuck them into our hearts. It's called safekeeping. I know. I've done that before. With you," he said, removing his hand from the car door and placing it on his chest. He covered his heart and then walked away.

Chapter 22

A week passed, and although they had not spoken to each other about how they were individually feeling, all three of them had contemplated making a move because something heavy had been weighing on each of their minds.

Gi received the divorce papers, and stalled with signing them until she spoke to Ric.

Lizzy drove by Hank Stewart's apartment twice, and swore to herself the next time she was going to stop, and knock on his door.

Kenzie made an appointment with her colleague, Dr. Brandy Kirchner at Lake Regional Health.

Kenzie skipped the part where she signed in and waited in the lobby for her name to be called. There was no nurse to take her blood pressure and ask her a few questions before sending in the doctor. Kenzie and Dr. Brandy Kirchner had become fast friends when Kenzie began working at the same hospital four years ago. Brandy was six years older, and Kenzie had always dubbed her *the wise one.* And right now, Kenzie was hoping her friend and colleague could ease her worry.

"Sit down, relax," Dr. Kirchner told Kenzie after they shared a brief hug in the the doorway of her office.

"This is driving me crazy, I thought you put a rush on the blood work?" Kenzie questioned her.

"It's only been twenty-four hours," Dr. Kirchner responded.

"And?" Kenzie asked her.

"It was positive. You're pregnant." Dr. Kirchner watched Kenzie's face fall. "I know this must be such a shock, and not having Peter here to share this with you has to be–"

"How far along am I?" Kenzie interrupted.

"Well that's difficult to determine without knowing the date of your last period. You told me you are prone to being irregular, right?" Dr. Kirchner asked.

"Yes, and with the strain of Peter's death, I just assumed my body was even more thrown off. I think I had a light period five or six weeks before the wedding," Kenzie tried to remember. She had gone off of her birth control pills when she and Peter got engaged – right before he was diagnosed with HD. The two of them had agreed to immediately start trying to conceive. Given Kenzie's irregularity, they wondered if it would take them awhile and had hoped it wouldn't be a challenge for them.

"I will schedule an ultrasound to give us the gestational age of the baby," Dr. Kirchner informed Kenzie. "It's also a good tool to reassure us that you have a healthy pregnancy."

Pregnancy. Was Kenzie hearing this right? She was going to pray very hard for this to be Peter's baby, conceived on their honeymoon – or earlier.

Lizzy circled around the block a second time. His truck was parked in the lot near his apartment. The idea of seeing Hank Stewart again had been on her mind, night and day. She would never know if this could have worked between them, if she didn't stop driving and go to him. This time, Lizzy didn't lose her nerve.

She knocked once on apartment number nine. She heard footsteps almost immediately on the other side of the door. When someone opened it, a woman –tall, thin, with long, red hair in loose curls all the way down her back– was standing there.

"Hi, can I help you?" she asked, and Lizzy wondered if Hank had moved. But again, his truck was parked out front.

"Yes, does Hank Stewart still live in this apartment?" Lizzy felt certain there was an easy explanation for this.

"He does, and he's in the shower right now." The woman was wearing short, frayed jeans shorts and a white v-neck t-shirt – and Lizzy didn't want to stare but at her first glance she thought she was braless.

Before Lizzy responded, a toddler, a girl, ran up behind the woman's bare leg and spoke, *mama*. And there it was. Lizzy had her explanation. *This woman was Hank's ex-wife and she had probably been there to drop off their daughter. She was just waiting for him to get out of the shower before she left.*

"Oh, you must be Hank's ex-wife?" Lizzy spoke, feeling better already as she chased away the assumption she almost made in her wild imagination about Hank and *this woman*.

"Um, yes," she responded, "but I'm hoping to reverse that very soon."

"Excuse me?" Lizzy asked for clarification even though she unfortunately already had understood.

"We're back together," the woman answered, "so if you're interested in him, you can leave now."

Lizzy took a few steps away from the open doorway and never looked back. She walked quickly to her vehicle and left there much faster than she came. There was no question in her mind. She had lost her chance with Hank Stewart.

Gi arrived unannounced at the apartment building where Ric had moved into when he left her. She had been there dozens of times already to pick up or drop off Suzie. But, this time was different. Ric wasn't expecting her.

She stood outside of the door for a moment, and listened. She could hear laughter. Her daughter's high-pitched giggle always could make her smile, no matter how she was feeling. Ric had a special bond with her, that was for certain. Gi could hear him talking, probably acting silly in an effort to get Suzie to eat her breakfast. She heard another voice too, followed by laughter that was unfamiliar to her.

There was instant silence on the other side of the door after she knocked. Gi waited, and Ric answered the door. He wore pajama pants that she didn't recognize, and no shirt. Her eyes went directly to the tattoo across his left breast that he also most definitely never had before.

"Gi, um, hi. You're early…unless I missed a text or something?" Ric looked back at the woman standing alongside the kitchen table where Suzie in her pajamas was sitting and exclaimed, *mommy*, while she kept eating her pancakes.

"No, I am early, I guess. Can I come in?" she asked, wanting to see this. Needing to put herself through it.

"Sure," Ric stepped back, again glancing at the woman in the kitchen. She was young, for sure. Her long blonde hair was pulled up into a messy knot on top of her head. She was wearing the matching shirt with Ric's pajama pants – with most likely nothing underneath. But Gi tried not to go there. She reminded herself of the laughter she had just heard. *They were happy.*

Gi's hair was once again hanging over her left eye, and as she moved her hand to brush it away, Ric spoke. "Gi, this is Hollie."

Hollie took the steps toward her, because at the moment Gi felt frozen. She could not move, or feel.

She forced herself to reach out her hand when she heard Hollie mention something about it being *so nice to meet her… she had heard so much about her.*

Really? was Gi's first and only thought.

Ric looked uncomfortable. Suzie was staring. Gi didn't want to embarrass herself or any of them.

"It's nice to meet you, too," she said, receiving Hollie's hand. "I don't want to interrupt your breakfast or your morning together. I just need to talk to you for one minute," Gi looked directly at Ric.

Suzie was still eating, and taking in the prospect of having all of those people she cared about most in this life – in the same room.

"Okay," he again looked at Hollie, before he suggested they go in Suzie's room. Gi was relieved not to be invited into his bedroom, because the very last thing she needed to add to this morning's agenda was the sight of their rumpled sheets on an unmade bed that very little slumber took place in.

Ric closed the door behind them in Suzie's room. Some of the toys Gi recognized, others she did not.

"I'm sorry, I know I'm intruding," she spoke, and again her eyes went to his newly tattooed boob.

"You're fine," he told her, and then he responded to her stare. "It was Hollie's idea." As Gi looked a little closer, she could make out a cursive H, somehow intertwined with a rose. She didn't need to analyze that. She only nodded her head, and then reached into her handbag on her shoulder.

"I signed the papers," she told him, and she handed them to him.

"Oh, that's good. Thank you." Her stalling for one week had concerned him a little.

"I just want to say something, if you'll hear me out," Gi spoke, and her voice was strong and in control, despite how she felt. "I needed to come here, to see this. This is your life now. Suzie talks about you –and Hollie– all the time, especially after she's with you for a night or a weekend. I know this is good for her. You're happy, and that's wonderful for you, too."

"Gi…" Ric started to speak. He wanted nothing more than for her to find happiness as well.

"No, don't," she told him. And that was just like her. Always wanting to be in control. He never could offer her a shoulder to cry on, without her insisting she was just fine. "I hope you'll always be this happy." She started to step past him. He had the divorce papers in his hands. She saw what she came for. It was all good. And now it was time for Gi to leave.

"You too," he stopped her, putting his hand on her upper arm. He gently tightened his grip around her bicep. For not working out a day in her life, Gi had muscle definition. "I want you to be happy, too. Allow yourself to be." Gi let those words sink in for a moment. *Allow yourself to be.*

"I hear you," she told him.

"We're friends now," he began. "We've never been friends before. It's good for us, a much better fit, don't you think?"

Gi smiled at him, she nodded her head in agreement with him, and then she touched the side of his scruffy cheek. "Friends. Sure. We've got this. See ya buddy," she said. And as she left, they both laughed.

Chapter 23

Lizzy was in the kitchen when she heard a door slam on the next level up. She immediately walked into the living room and stood at the base of the stairway. "Griffin? What's going on?" It took two more loud calls of her son's name before he appeared at the top of those stairs. Looking up there, Lizzy felt a wave of remorse, recalling what happened that night, the final night of Max's life. She wondered again how long she and her son would continue to live there. It may be time to downsize, Max was the one who insisted they live big.

"I asked you what's going on," she said again as he only stood up there, looking down at her.

"I'm pissed, okay?" he stated, as his rare preteen attitude surfaced.

"Watch your language, and come down here and tell me why!" Lizzy ordered him.

When Griffin reached the base of the stairs, Lizzy asked him to follow her into the kitchen, where she had just started cooking their dinner.

Griffin didn't sit down as Lizzy checked the boiling water on the stovetop.

"I've been talking to Trey every night since he went back to Boston," Griffin told her. "He had some news tonight." Lizzy could see how something had really upset her son. She kept silent and waited to hear what it was. "He's always wanted to teach abroad. He said he applied over a year ago. Well, he's been accepted and he's considering it. That means he'll be gone for an entire year! How can he do this to me? I just lost dad, and I wanted my new dad, my real dad, -whatever the hell I am supposed to call him- in my life!" Griffin was near tears, and Lizzy rushed to turn off the burner on the stovetop, and then she reached for him. He wouldn't let her comfort him. He backed away in anger.

"Grif, this doesn't sound like a done deal yet. Calm down. I'm sure after Trey gives it some thought, he will realize he can't accept it." Lizzy was in disbelief that Trey even shared the tentative news with Griffin. She thought of it as irresponsible of him, and it angered her, too.

"He said it's a chance of a lifetime. A school in Barcelona, Spain wants him. He'll possibly be getting involved with the Euroleague basketball there. There's so much he kept talking about, and the more he talked I could tell how much he wanted to go. How can he leave now, Mom? I thought Boston was far enough away, but now Europe?"

This time Griffin started to cry, and Lizzy enveloped him into her arms. He may have been twelve years old, and almost as tall as her five-eight frame already, but he was still just a boy. He was hurting from his father's death, and now Trey was breaking his heart, too. *This was exactly what Lizzy had warned Trey not to do.*

"Please talk to him, mom," Griffin begged her.

"What am I going to say to change his mind?" she asked, knowing they were still so very much like strangers, and probably always would be.

"I don't know? Anything! Just convince him to stay in the country." Griffin stood there with tears pooling in his eyes again, and Lizzy told him she would try.

✱

When Griffin was in the shower before bed, Lizzy called Trey in Boston. He answered on the second ring.

"What are you thinking?" she instantly asked him.

"I knew you would call," he said, taking in a deep breath. "It's the chance of a lifetime. I'm torn. But, come on, this doesn't happen to people every day."

"I remember you saying something very similar to me when I told you that I was pregnant. You wanted to pursue your basketball scholarship and college career," Lizzy stated, coldly.

"That's not fair," Trey replied in the phone.

"The hell it isn't! If you do this, you will be abandoning him again. Only this time, your son is old enough to understand – and he'll know better than to ever forgive you." Lizzy showed him no mercy. She shouldn't have cared less if he traveled the globe and never returned. But, for Griffin, she had to care. And she did.

"Technology is amazing for keeping in touch. Nothing has to change. We can still talk daily, we can continue to get to know each other better. We will just have to postpone dinner and other visits until I'm back." Trey sounded as if his decision had already been made.

"Long distance is tough enough on people who have solid relationships," she told him. "The two of you are just now starting to piece together yours. How can you leave him, especially now that he just lost the only father he's ever known?"

"The timing of this sucks so bad," Trey said on the other end of the phone, and Lizzy could hear that eighteen-year-old boy in his voice again.

"Don't make me single-handedly pick up the pieces alone again," Lizzy told him. "I know I can manage, but I'm not so sure about our son."

Chapter 24

Kenzie answered her cell phone on the third ring. She had been lying down on one end of the sectional and had fallen asleep in her pitch-dark living room. She wanted a drink badly, but she knew she couldn't. The amount of alcohol she already had consumed in recent weeks concerned her to no end. She had no idea how long she'd been pregnant. Or whose baby she was carrying.

"Hello," she said, thinking Trey was the last person she needed to talk to right now. She couldn't tell him, and she wouldn't. Not until she knew for sure.

"Hey, did I wake you?" Trey asked, recognizing that she sounded half asleep.

"Yeah, but it's okay," she told him, "I only closed my eyes for a few minutes."

"I have something I want to talk to you about. I've hurt Griffin's feelings and ticked off Lizzy pretty badly," Trey explained.

"What in the world did you do?" Kenzie asked him, suddenly feeling more awake.

"I've been accepted to teach abroad for a year…" he stated, cautiously.

"Oh my God…you cannot go. You can't leave Griffin!" Kenzie's mind was racing. If he was her baby's father, he would be leaving this child too. Just like he had abandoned Lizzy and his baby on the way. *Kenzie vowed to pray harder that this baby was Peter's.*

"I am torn," he admitted, and Kenzie could definitely hear the distraught emotion in his voice. "I'm thinking of us, too," he added.

"There is no us, Trey," she replied, sighing, and wondering if she really should push him away now. If he was this baby's father, they could be together. A family. Kenzie wasn't ready for any of this.

"You keep saying that, but I know you don't believe it. Not with all of your heart," Trey spoke, entirely too confident.

"Stop putting feelings into my heart," she said, and then she smiled at how funny those words sounded strung together.

"That could be a song or something," he teased, and she giggled on the other end of the phone.

"Hang up and ponder your future, Toennies," she told him.

"Okay, but I called to get your opinion," he said, hoping to keep her on the phone talking to him for a few more minutes. He liked hearing the sound of her voice. He could imagine where she was sitting…and what she was wearing this late at night.

"You didn't call to get my perspective," she stated. "You already know I will think you are the world's biggest dick all over again if you leave another time!"

"Are you making reference to the memory of seeing me naked?" he teased her.

"Haha…goodnight, Trey."

✽

Gi shifted the gear of her burnt orange jeep into park. She hadn't been there in well over year. It was funny though, no matter how much time had passed, she still thought the place looked the same. Other trailers had been replaced with newer models, but not her mother's. She still played house in the same, rundown trailer which had too much mold growing on it to be able to tell what color it was originally.

She got out of her jeep, and walked up the uneven concrete pavers that had overgrown grass overtop of most of them.

After loudly knocking once, Gi heard her mother yell, *it's open!* So she turned the knob and went in.

"Well I'll be damned!" her mother called out, and Gi spotted her petite frame standing in the kitchen, wearing a dingy white night gown. Her once auburn hair had a considerable amount of gray. It was stringy-looking as it reached her shoulders. The cigarette hanging out of her mother's mouth instantly annoyed Gi.

"I thought you quit smoking?" she asked, remembering a year ago she had been wearing a nicotine patch and claimed to be feeling like a new woman after giving up cigarettes.

"Three weeks! That's how long it lasted. I was doing fine until I brought a gentleman home. You gotta smoke after sex."

"Oh please, mother. Spare me." And that was why Gi had stayed away from this woman. From the time she was a little girl to the present, Dixie Hunter was a bad influence.

"Hey a woman's gotta get some enjoyment out of life," she told her daughter. "What are you doing for fun these days?

I heard about your divorce. I guess you're like your mama after all – when it comes to hanging onto a man."

Shut up! Gi wanted so badly to scream at her, but she refrained. She was better than that. It was her choice to come there today. Her conscious decision to see her mother again. "We weren't good for each other," Gi attempted to explain, but wondered if she should bother.

"Is he a part of that little girl's life?" That little girl had a name, but Dixie had never wanted any part of being a grandmother to Suzie.

"Yes, he's great, very hands-on," Gi offered.

"Good," Dixie answered, extinguishing the cigarette butt in the ashtray on the middle of the table. *Did anyone still use indoor ashtrays?* "Why are you here?" Her question was direct and unfeeling, but Gi expected nothing less.

"I want you to tell me how to be happy," Gi spoke sincerely.

"You're asking me?" Dixie scoffed.

"Yes. You should know me best. You raised me. When did I stop being happy? Why do I not allow myself to be?" This was what it had come to. Gi was back to where it all started. At her mother's house. The place where Gi had learned to fend for herself in every aspect of life. Inside those paneled walls, she had never felt more alone.

Dixie stared at her for a long time before she spoke. "You really are struggling? The daughter who I've always known to be stronger, more successful, and more level-headed than I'll ever be? It's time to see yourself as others do." Gi prepared herself for a verbal beating. Again, she expected to be compared to her loser of a mother. And lately, Gi had felt like the failure she believed her mother to be. Allowing her marriage to fail had taken a terrible toll on her. Especially when she witnessed how quickly Ric found happiness. She used to fault him for her misery. Now, she wondered if she was the one who made them unhappily married.

"Whenever you have failed, you blamed me," her mother acknowledged, "and when you succeeded you compared yourself to me. You patted yourself on the back after any triumph because you believed that proved you were nothing like me. There's been some sort of tug of war going on inside of you for your entire life. Stop bringing me into your highs and lows. It's time to let it be. Yes, I sucked as a mother. You have already made up for that in spades by being the best mother in the world to your little girl. You don't need me to tell you that. You already know that. The kind of person you are, well you're… just like your father."

Gi was still taking in all that she had heard come out of her mother's mouth, and possibly even straight from her heart. It took her a moment to realize what also her mother had said. *She was just like her father?*

"I never knew my father. I don't even know his name. You gave me and my brother your name. We were Hunters. You said he left before I was born." The direction this conversation had taken caught Gi completely off guard.

"You and your brother have different fathers. Your brother's father ended up in prison for drugs and later when he was let out, he overdosed and died. Your father, on the other hand, was not my usual kind of company that I like to keep, if you know what I mean." Dixie paused to cough. The sound of that smoker's hack brought Gi back to her childhood. That was why she never touched a cigarette in her lifetime. She used to lie awake in her bed at night, wall to wall with her mother's bedroom, so afraid she was going to cough herself to death. It sounded awful then, and still did now.

"Who was he?" Gi felt her own hands begin to tremble.

"A man of integrity. I never once held it against him that he didn't claim you. He couldn't. He had a family of his own, and a prominent career. I didn't want to be the one to ruin that for him, nor did I want to be scorned like that. People are way too judgy in this town." Gi could have rolled her eyes. Her mother hardly would have surprised anyone as an adulteress.

"Did he offer to support me at all?" Gi remembered all too well the times there was hardly any food in the house. To this day, she could not stomach peanut butter and jelly. And she never once fed that to her own daughter.

"Oh yeah, he wrote a check here and there…but I never spent any of the money on you." *Oh dear God. This was her mother. Dixie Hunter defined selfish.*

"So my father was some sort of pillar in the community? Did I know him?" Gi was not leaving there until she at least found out his name. Something she never cared about before was suddenly very important to her.

"You used to come home from the elementary school and tell me stories about your teachers, the secretaries, and the principal. You never missed a thing that went on in the building. You were a little busy body. A few times you were sent to the principal's office because you were acting too tough for your own good. Remember Mr. Reid, who could be stern, but he would never punish you?"

"Mr. Reid retired and was elected the mayor of Lake Ozark, but he had a heart attack and died before he finished his term." As Gi recalled this history, she stopped talking. "Was he my–?"

"I was only with him one time. And what a gentleman he was."

Gi stood there in awe. Mr. James Reid was the first male in her life she ever remembered respecting. He used to tossel her hair in the hallway, and it always made her smile. Maybe he did that to all of the students? She once believed that anyway. Now, she wanted to think of it as his way of showing affection to only her. He was wrong not to claim her as a child, but Gi wasn't angry. There was no point to be now.

"I really liked that man," Gi told her mother.

"Yeah, I know…and he really liked you."

Gi turned to face the direction of the door which she had not been standing too far from throughout this entire conversation. She felt overwhelmed and she wanted to escape from there and think.

"Yes, you go," her mother read her mind. "And remember, you are a successful business woman, a wonderful mother, and a loyal friend. You're just like your father."

When Dixie finished speaking, she lit up another cigarette between her fingers.

And before Gi walked out, she replied, "Thanks, mom."

Chapter 25

"Mr. Reid from Lake Ozark Elementary was your father?" Kenzie asked, feeling complete disbelief, and Lizzy was speechless.

Again, the three of them were gathered around the island in Lizzy's kitchen. It had been too long since they were together. And since, they had each gone through quite a bit of crazy in their lives.

"I still can't believe it," Gi sighed. "Who would have thought? I have decent, civilized blood pumping through my veins."

"So you're not thinking of him as scum for never claiming you as his daughter?" Lizzy asked, but she already knew what Gi's answer would be. That scenario was too familiar in their lives – and none of them had ever truly *hated* Trey Toennies.

"Who knew Griffin and I would have something like that in common!" Gi laughed.

"Only your daddy isn't coming back for you," Kenzie stated, in a respectable way. "He died of a heart attack when he was our mayor, didn't he?"

"I remember that, too," Lizzy stated.

"I think we all do," Gi told them. "He was just the kind of man who was such a staple, you know? I mean, wouldn't we all like to be someone who people remember and miss long after we are gone?"

"I don't know," Lizzy responded. "I think I would rather be loved and missed by the people closest to me than to have total strangers or people who just knew of me, thinking of me or remembering me. That's not important to me."

"I can see it both ways," Kenzie chimed in.

"That's only because you want a hospital wing named after you in years to come," Gi teased, and they all laughed.

And then Gi spoke again. "So I guess the reason I called our meeting tonight was to tell you two that I've finally gotten some closure. My divorce is final, I'm happy for Ric who's happy with Hollie and they've included my daughter in their happy little circle. I've also been able to let go of blaming myself for my failed marriage. I am not my mother. Apparently I am my father. And, as strange as this does sound, I'm proud of the truth."

"That is so odd," Kenzie stated, "but it makes sense. I'm really happy for you, Gi. You deserve to have found peace."

"Yes!" Gi agreed, "Now, let's drink to that!"

Lizzy jumped up from her stool to retrieve a bottle of wine from the refrigerator and three glasses from the cabinet.

"None for me, thanks," Kenzie stated immediately.

"Why?" both Lizzy and Gi asked simultaneously.

"I'm just detoxing again," she was quick to answer.

"Don't be ridiculous!" Lizzy told her. "Just have one with us." Kenzie allowed Lizzy to pour her a glass, but she planned to let it sit untouched in front of her. She knew by the end of this night, her friends would know the truth anyway. It was time to confide in them. She was going crazy keeping her pregnancy to herself.

"You're going to want to drink after I tell you the latest with Trey," Lizzy said as she took a long swallow from her glass before she even sat down again.

"Now what?" Gi asked, and Kenzie already knew. She was still thinking about Trey's late-night phone call.

"As if Boston wasn't far enough for Trey, he's now been offered to teach abroad," Lizzy said, still feeling miffed about the fact that he was even considering it. She understood his desire to apply for the job when he wasn't in Griffin's life. But now, so much had changed. It irked her to think he didn't see Griffin as a reason not to go. "He's considering moving to Barcelona, Spain for an entire year."

"Holy shit!" Gi exclaimed, and Kenzie kept quiet because this came as no surprise to her tonight.

"Yes, my thoughts exactly," Lizzy sighed.

"How's Grif handling this?" Kenzie asked, because she honestly did not know anything more than what Trey had told her, which was that he had hurt Griffin's feelings.

"Not well," Lizzy replied. "He continues to talk to Trey every day after school, and he hasn't said too much to me lately about what's going on. He's so moody at times. I'm leaving the subject off the table until this weekend. We are going to sit down together with Trey and talk this out."

That was something Kenzie did not know. "He's coming home again this weekend?"

"Yes, his idea. Something tells me he has already made up his mind to go and he only wants to smooth things over with Griffin. I don't know. I think he's an asshole if he leaves his son again." Lizzy would not show him any mercy this time. She was certain of that.

"He told me that he's torn," Kenzie admitted.

"He did?" Lizzy asked. "So, he called you or something?"

"Yes, the same night he broke the news to Griffin," Kenzie stated, and she noticed Gi was looking at her with an odd expression on her face.

"Are you two talking like friends again?" Lizzy inquired, and again Gi kept quiet but watched Kenzie very closely.

"Not really," Kenzie replied. "Would that bother you if we did though?"

"I guess not," Lizzy said, feeling confused at best. And maybe a little jealous.

"Seriously, you two!" Gi finally spoke. "Don't even go there again. Battling over Trey Toennies is ancient history. Isn't it?"

"We never really battled over him," Kenzie said, looking at Lizzy. "You just slept with my boyfriend and then my relationship with him went up in flames."

"And now it's my turn to shock you, twelve years later," Kenzie carefully spoke of what she came there to share with those two tonight. "I slept with Trey when he was in town."

Gi choked on the wine she had just sipped. And Lizzy never moved or spoke a word.

"Please, just hear me first," Kenzie continued. "I was alone and drinking in my condo. I never asked him to stop by. I never reached out to him in any way. He stopped by to thank me for talking to you and sort of helping to bring Griffin back into his life. I really didn't do anything to encourage that, and I told him so."

"Was that before or after you took off your panties for him?" Lizzy interjected with a serious pissed off tone.

"Stop," Gi told her. "Hear her out."

Kenzie continued. "I am so lonely without Peter. I'm sad and distraught and I was drinking excessively. Trey was there. It was a moment of *help me forget, let me feel something other than grief.*"

Gi completely sympathized and understood, but Lizzy continued to let her anger build. "Is this your way of getting back at me?" Lizzy asked her with obvious pain in her eyes.

"What? No! Of course not! That's childish of you to even think it!" Kenzie defended herself as she implied that Lizzy needed to grow up.

"Is there more?" Gi asked. "Was it a one-night stand, or are you two pursuing a relationship?"

"I told him I am not interested," Kenzie said, looking down at her full glass of wine.

"Is that the truth?" Lizzie asked her.

"It has to be. I'm still grieving for my husband, and now I have a bigger issue that has pushed its way front and center into my life." Kenzie looked at Gi first, and then back at Lizzy. Gi looked at the untouched wine glass in front of her best friend. She knew her well. And she also feared how Lizzy was going to react to what she revealed next. Gi assumed Kenzie was pregnant with Trey's baby.

Kenzie finished what she had wanted to tell them, what she at times had thought about confiding in them individually. "I'm pregnant."

Lizzy covered her mouth with her hand and started to cry. *This was like a nightmare for her. What was happening to her life?*

"Does Trey know?" Gi was the first to ask.

"No," Kenzie answered. "This could be Peter's baby." And that's when she released the emotion that had been building inside of her for days. She had not allowed herself to cry, or to speak of it. Because that would make it all too real. Gi was quick to envelop Kenzie into her arms as she sobbed. And then Gi glared at Lizzy. This was not who they were. They supported each other through anything, no matter what.

Lizzy stood up and while she had wanted to leave the room and go slam a few doors or throw something until it broke, she stepped around to the opposite side of the island and stood arms-length away from her friends. Kenzie's pain was utterly heartbreaking. The father of her child was one of two – either dead, or leaving the country.

Lizzy could relate to Kenzie's heartbreak, as she reached out and held her while she cried continued to cry.

"It's going to be okay," Lizzy whispered.

"How do you know that?" Kenzie asked her, through her tears.

"I think I can answer that," Gi spoke up. "It's simple, really. When the three of us are together, supporting and loving each other as we always have, it just feels like everything will be okay. It's always been like that." Gi was the first to place her hand palm down on the island. Lizzy was next. And finally, Kenzie touched their hands with hers.

No one said it, but they were all thinking the same.

Trinity.

Chapter 26

When Trey arrived in Lake Ozark early on Saturday morning, Griffin and Lizzy were his first stop.

Lizzy watched her son barrel down the stairs and run straight to the front door. She stood back and momentarily held her breath. If Trey was going to disappoint her son, she would never forgive him this time.

The two of them exchanged words, and Lizzy inevitably felt left out. It was almost as if she was going to be the last to know something.

Trey greeted her too, and she invited him into the kitchen for homemade cinnamon rolls. It was an afterthought, but Lizzy figured he hadn't eaten anything that fattening in a very long time. She smiled to herself, thinking how poor Griffin was going to be a chunky monkey like her. Neither one of them could resist good food that was not-so-good for them.

After they ate, Lizzy was the first to bring up the subject they were gathered together for this morning. "Out with it," she told Trey. "What have you decided to do? Are you staying in Boston, or leaving your son again?"

That wasn't fair and Lizzy knew it, but she didn't feel at all ashamed. Griffin looked down at the tabletop in front of him. Trey let Lizzy's words go. He knew she was partly right. And he understood her reason to be angry.

"Yes, I've made a decision about my life and what I want to do with it for the next year," Trey said, and Lizzy was blatantly reminded of his inexperience as a parent. Her life had not been her own since Griffin was born. For Lizzy, in reference to anything, *my* life was *their* life. "I accepted the job."

Lizzy was sure she had heard him wrong. She was flabbergasted by his selfishness, but she cursed herself for thinking Trey had matured and changed. Her first and only concern now was her son. Lizzy looked at Griffin, and he did not appear surprised or at all disappointed.

"So that's it? You're off to fulfill yet another dream? Do you have any idea what you're walking away from – again?" Lizzy focused on her son and then on Trey.

"Griffin knows nothing changes between us," Trey told her. "In fact, this opportunity could bring us closer."

"Do you hear yourself?" Lizzy asked, utterly disgusted by him.

"After his first six months there, I want to join him," Griffin revealed, and Lizzy felt lightheaded.

"Excuse me?" she asked her son to clarify the craziness that just came from his mouth, or his brain. It hadn't appeared as if he was utilizing it though.

"I can go to school there. I'll also be able to be a part of the Euroleague. Mom, playing basketball in Spain would be so awesome!"

Lizzy didn't think twice. She simply said no. To both of them.

"Mom!" Griffin protested. "Have an open mind!"

"Go upstairs to your room," she told him.

"But I'm a part of this conversation – and this decision!" Griffin tried again.

"Now," she told him without raising her voice. One look. That's all it ever took sometimes from a mother to her child. Griffin got up abruptly from the table and stormed upstairs to his bedroom.

Lizzy waited for the door to slam before she spoke. "You just saw and heard my son's reaction to me parenting him. He wasn't happy, but he listened. I am in control of his life for as long as he is a child. I make the decisions that are in his best interest."

"Then why did you just make a decision based solely on what you want?" Trey boldly asked her. "No mother wants to ship off her son halfway around the world for six months. You would have disappointed me if you had initially said yes. But now, you need to set aside what you want, and consider how your son would benefit from going to school abroad – and nurturing a newfound relationship with a father he's never known. He's almost a teenager. Max is gone. He needs a male in his life. I need him in my life. Think of Griffin. Think long and hard before you say no – for certain."

"Go to hell," Lizzy told him, and she said those harsh words not because she was adamantly standing by her original decision. But because she knew Trey was right.

Chapter 27

The three of them sat in an empty waiting area outside of Dr. Brandy Kirchner's obstetrics and gynecology office. The frosted sliding glass window was closed between the office and the waiting area. No one was around to overhear them, as Kenzie spoke openly.

"This just has to be Peter's baby," she sighed, blinking back the tears that started to pool in her eyes.

"You have no idea, at all?" Gi asked her. "I mean if you have been pregnant for awhile, there weren't any signs that seemed odd to you? Weight gain? Bloating? Sore boobs?"

"None of that, Dr. Gi," Kenzie smiled, and Lizzy giggled.

"I'm worried about the drinking you did if you were pregnant for weeks following Peter's death," Lizzy said, as if Kenzie need to be reminded. That fact was scaring her more than the baby's paternity.

"Yes, you and me both, but Dr. Kirchner told me not to panic. For years, women were told not to touch a drop of alcohol. Apparently new studies have shown during the first trimester, alcohol intake doesn't appear to increase complications for the baby. I didn't just have a drink or two though, so there's the risk for the baby to have Fetal Alcohol Syndrome." Kenzie looked hopeless when she added, "If only I had known."

"One step at a time," Gi told her. "This could be Trey's baby, which will mean you're not that far along."

"That's possible, he could have impregnated me... holy smokes that night was hot," Kenzie giggled, and Gi joined her.

"Hush your mouth," Lizzy told her. "I do not want to hear this. I mean, come on, the both of you repeatedly steered me clear of having mind-blowing sex and I listened! I had my chance and I let it pass me by. Why am I the one missing out?" All three of them laughed out loud – Lizzy too, because she knew she had to let that fantasy go.

"I still don't think you've seen the last of Hank," Kenzie stated, with a little hope in her heart for her best friend.

"Oh yes I have. I'm not going to be the one to hunt him down. I'm certain of that. How embarrassing!" Lizzy sunk lower in her chair, and cringed at the recollection.

*

Kenzie was lying on a gurney. Her shirt was raised and the doctor was applying a warm gel to her lower abdomen. The room was dim-lit and the computer monitor near her feet would momentarily detect the life growing inside of her. Kenzie was nervous, and on each side of her stood both Gi and Lizzy. She needed them to be with her when she received the news.

*

When it was over, the lights were turned back on, and Dr. Kirchner had already left the exam room. Lizzy had gone over to a chair along the wall to sit down, and Gi was pacing around a little in a room with limited space. It was Kenzie who appeared to handle the news the best of the three of them.

Chapter 28

The waves from the Pacific Ocean reached the beach, and their bare feet. Toes in the smooth white sand, drinks in hand, and the hot sun on their bodies. Two years had passed and life as Gi, Kenzie and Lizzy had known – changed yet again. The only constant, and it had always been that way for them, was having each other.

Three, thirty-year-old women sat in a half circle stance, toes nearly touching. They all were solemn and quiet, and it was Kenzie who needed to speak of it. "I'm looking at this sand, and it's a mixture of white and yellow colors with a finely grated texture that I can feel seeping between my toes. And every once in a while there's a pebble or a rock mixed within. But you know what else? For me, there's life in it, too. The ashes of an amazing man who I was given only limited time with. I'm still not over the unfairness of it, but I'm at least at peace with moving on."

"But isn't it amazing how his life carries on, even though he's not really here?" Lizzy attempted to explain. "That's how I've always thought of my mother. She's the constant whisper in my ear – especially all the times I've done something wrong in my life. And believe me, there were many times I wish she had stopped me. I can hear her in my own laughter. I see her in the funny little way Griffin bites the inside of his cheek when he's anxious or deep in thought. Peter will always be here in many kinds of ways, too."

Kenzie was smiling at Lizzy's description of something she now understood perfectly. Gi turned her head. Suzie was attempting to build a sand castle. It was her first time at the beach, first experience seeing the ocean. She was seven years old, and already beginning to lose her childlike qualities. Her legs and torso were long and lean. Her cheeks were far less round and chubby. Her hair was now considerably shorter in the back and longer on top, just like Gi's. She was filling small buckets with sand, packing them full, while a two-year-old little boy with brown wavy hair watched closely her every move.

"PJ," Kenzie called out to the little boy beside Suzie. "No, no. Do not eat the sand. Just play." It was also Peter Jack's first time in the sand in Maui. He was a spitting image of his daddy. His mannerisms, too. Smart, goofy enough at times to generate laughter, and he already seized life as if he knew exactly how precious every single moment was.

"Who would have thought the first time you were ready to come back here, you would have a part of Peter in tow," Gi noted. "Ahh, it's so amazing how life works."

Lizzy turned her head and saw Griffin, sitting in the sand a short distance away. His knees were bent on his long legs. His fourteen-year-old body had suddenly grown into a man. His regular vigorous workouts with his father, in an attempt to keep his son in the best the shape for his pending high school basketball career, were paying off. His shoulders were broad, his chest was thick, and his once blubberish stomach had turned into hard muscle. Lizzy watched him. He was talking, or maybe that was his attempt at flirting, with two teenage girls in skimpy bikinis. One of them tossled his thick dark hair and Lizzy saw him blush. *Ahhh the awkward days of being a teenager with raging hormones. For Lizzy, she was relieved that trying time in her life was long behind her.*

"Does that boy not know he's better off leaving well enough alone?" Gi asked, subtly referring to romantic relationships, and both Kenzie and Lizzy completely understood.

"He'll have to learn that on his own, just like we all did," Lizzy stated.

"We do suck at those relationships," Kenzie partly teased.

"Well you didn't," Gi told Kenzie. "You were just dealt a shitty hand."

"Ah yes, and your husband fell to his death too…" Kenzie said, turning to Lizzy.

"Not quite like yours did," Lizzy replied, and her eyes widened at memory of Max's fall hardly being an accident. They could laugh about it. It was the only way to deal sometimes.

"At least yours still had his pants up," Gi said to Kenzie, in reference to Lizzy's asshole of a husband. They all laughed out loud in unison, and among their roaring laughter one of them said, *we are bad*.

They may have been a little shocking in their ways. But their choices at times during their lives had never altered their character. It's who they were as individuals that had initially drawn them to each other as children – and it was most definitely who they were as *trinity* that saw them through it all.

And there was more to come.

Epilogue

Griffin, Suzie, and PJ came together in a group hug. It's what they did whenever they were reunited. So much of their childhoods were spent in each other's lives – because of their mothers. A closeness between anyone cannot be forged nor forced, but for those three children it was effortless to care about each other after they had witnessed firsthand the special connection among Gi, Kenzie, and Lizzy. Through it all, they observed how their mothers loved, supported, and stood by each other during every aspect of their lives.

Griffin and Suzie were now in their seventies, and PJ had reached his sixties. Their mothers were all three ninety years old when they died.

Their mature adult children stood in the back of a church in Lake Ozark. Soon, they would proceed to the front and sit down with their families in the pews. Today they were celebrating, not mourning, three women whose lives were well-lived. None of them ever had additional children after they each bore one. And neither of the three had ever remarried.

For ***Lizzy***, Hank Stewart did find his way back into her life. He offered her what no man had ever been able to. *True romantic love, and an undeniable physical chemistry.* Her happiness with him had lasted nearly sixty years. Hank not only fulfilled a dream for her, but he encouraged Lizzy to purse anything she may have ever thought she could be. At age thirty-three, Lizzy had gone to college for the first time in her life, and eventually earned a Registered Nursing degree. Just like her mother. She then worked as a nurse at Lake Regional Health for twenty years.

For ***Gi***, her focus became clearer. As a business woman in a city that continued to flourish, she recognized that it was not only feasible, but gratifying for her to give back. She was the driving force between creating grants in the local schools, earned and presented in her father's name. Gi also ran for Mayor of Lake Ozark when she was in her fifties, and she had spent an entire decade serving the same city her father had. No one, except for those closest to her, ever knew the truth behind her inspiration. *Principal James Reid.* Gi also had rediscovered herself after her divorce from Ric. And she had spent most of her adult years in a solid, loving relationship with her partner, Nikki.

For ***Kenzie***, her life was the most challenging. Her son, Peter Jack had been born with partial Fetal Alcohol Syndrome. It was a disorder that was irreversible, and PJ was most affected with neurodevelopment issues. Mild to moderate learning difficulties plagued him as a baby and a toddler, which continued in school and throughout most of his life. PJ also been diagnosed in his fifties with Huntington's Disease. He, however, was the only male in his family who did not succumb to the disease. Doctors had discovered that his symptoms were slow to progress. And, for that, Kenzie was grateful. She certainly had not gone through life unscathed. Despite her pain and her struggles, Kenzie recognized her blessings. Without Peter, she never would have had PJ, her only son. Without PJ, she never would have known unconditional love and become the compassionate person she had. Through the years of her medical career, Kenzie utilized her position to spread knowledge and raise money for continuous research for both Fetal Alcohol Syndrome and Huntington's Disease. She became a keynote speaker at numerous workshops and conventions across the country for decades of her medical career and throughout her retirement. Her friends were proud of her, her colleagues admired her, and Trey Toennies had been by her side, encouraging her and loving her.

Gi, Lizzy, and **Kenzie** had been born to find each other. A higher power ensured they would spend their whole lives together. And they had. Right up until their deaths, precisely three consecutive days apart. *Natural causes, old age.* Nothing else could be attributed. But their families knew. One simply could not exist without the other.

As the priest near the altar raised his hand and made the sign of the cross, he spoke, "God the father, his son, and Holy Spirit."

"Well said," Griffin stated aloud, as he turned around from the front pew to make eye contact with both Suzie and PJ. And they all were clearly thinking the same thing.

Trinity.

ABOUT THE AUTHOR

One quote. *"Maybe our girlfriends are our soulmates, and guys are just people to have fun with."* That's what inspired me to write Trinity.

Most of my readers are women. I wanted to write a story that celebrates us and those irreplaceable friendships. We all get it. We understand what it means to have those friends – who are there during the 'just because' moments, and always there to support us through anything. Friendships are far from perfect, but it's those imperfections that draw us together and relate us on a level all its own. For Gi, Kenzie, and Lizzy, in this story they were trinity – three closely related people. The state of being three was how they lived their lives, and survived it all.

The laughter. The tears. The misunderstandings. The hurt. The encouragement. The honesty (especially when we don't want to hear it). The drinks. The hugs. The memories. I almost do not have the words to describe what my closest friends mean to me. We weren't born related, or with lives already intertwined, but we were meant to find each other.

For all of my people. And your people too. Friendship is one of life's greatest blessings. Recognize, savor, and cherish your beautiful bonds.

As always, thank you for reading!

Love,

Lori Bell

Made in the USA
Lexington, KY
11 February 2017